THE WANDERER

*OTHER TITLES BY MONICA EDWARDS IN THE
ARMADA SERIES INCLUDE*

BLACK HUNTING WHIP
NO MISTAKING CORKER
PUNCHBOWL HARVEST
THE COWNAPPERS
THE OUTSIDER
FIRE IN THE PUNCHBOWL

The Wanderer was first published in
the U.K. in 1953 by William Collins
Sons & Co. Ltd, London and Glasgow.
This edition was first published in 1968
by May Fair Books Ltd, 14 St. James's
Place, London, S.W.1, and was printed in
Great Britain by Love & Malcomson Ltd,
Brighton Road, Redhill, Surrey.

MONICA EDWARDS

The Wanderer

COVER ILLUSTRATION BY
MARY GERNATT

TEXT ILLUSTRATIONS BY
JOAN WANKLYN

Armada

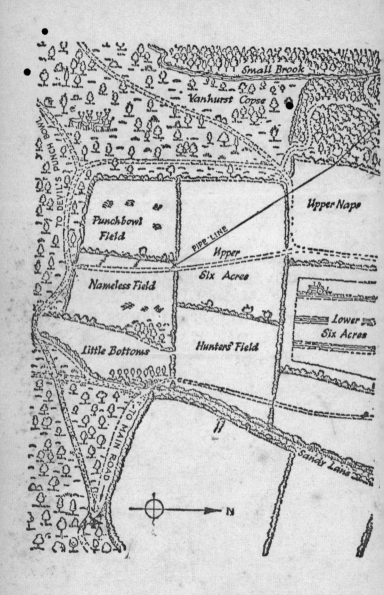

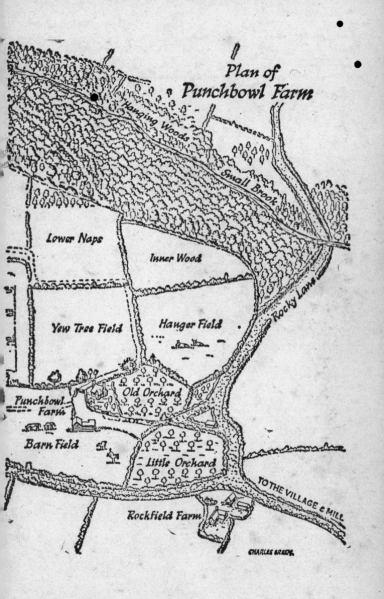

Plan of
Punchbowl Farm

Hanging Woods

Small Brook

Lower Naps

Inner Wood

Rocky Lane

Yew Tree Field

Hanger Field

Old Orchard

Punchbowl Farm

Barn Field

Little Orchard

TO THE VILLAGE & MILL

Rockfield Farm

CHARLES GREEN.

CHAPTER ONE

Six Dark Red Jewels

DION and Lindsey were now hardly on speaking terms. The night was black and sodden, and the rain poured down on Dion's still unfamiliar spectacles so that, as far as vision was concerned, he might just as well have been walking on the bottom of the sea. He was, in fact, walking on the bottom of the Devil's Punch Bowl, his sister somewhere close behind him and the wind and rain whirling blackly all around them.

"The devil's having dragon's-blood broth in his bowl tonight," Lindsey said, half hoping to improve the hostile situation between them. It was bad enough tramping heavy-legged through the clutching fingers of wet heather, looking for the heifers and the colt, when everyone else was probably having supper by the fire, without the added misery of Dion's annoyance with her. He didn't even answer her now, though of course he might not have heard, in the racket of the storm. She could see the black shine of his rubber boots thrusting through the tall drenched heather in the circle of his torchlight. His stride was too long and too fast for her, crunching in the brown, dead bracken stalks and rattling the loose stones. Her own wellingtons felt so heavily resistant that she began to imagine she was slowly dying from the feet upwards—from drowning, of course, because of all the water that came beating on her face and running coldly down her neck. A sou'wester didn't stop that; the rain soaked her short ends of hair, ran round her jawbone and surged triumphantly into the crack between her collar and her neck.

"Hell's bells and buckets of blood!" said Dion suddenly, his torch swinging madly like a mast-head light in a gale. Lindsey stopped and stared, and even the sight of Dion fighting a bramble bush could not quite eclipse the glorious swift relief of not lifting one foot after the other.

"Oh, rotten luck!" she said, stuffing the wet rope of her halter under the other arm and stretching out a hand. "I suppose the torch isn't really much use, with those spectacles."

"No more use than headlights with a wet windscreen."

Ignoring her hand, he trampled and tore his way out from the clutches of the bramble.

"Mightn't it be better with them off?" Lindsey suggested, forcing herself to walk on again behind him.

"Couldn't see a thing then—oh, I don't know—I suppose it can't be much worse than it is now."

He stopped again, and Lindsey watched the sideways incline of his sou'wester as he took the glasses off and stowed them, in their case, inside his pocket. "At least I shan't lose or break the darned things so easily now."

If Lindsey had hoped, from these unhostile remarks, for a return of their old familiar friendliness she couldn't have been much more mistaken. To Dion, struggling against the unaccustomed handicap of poor eyesight and worried about the two heifers and the colt so near the busy Portsmouth road, the bramble bush was almost the last straw.

"Look here, Lin, we've been out since before sunset: two hours at least. What's the use? We can't hope to find them in all this. I'm going home."

"But what about the main road? They might be killed before morning; we must find them! I'll try calling them again."

Dion tore a bramble stem from his trouser-leg and flung it into the black wind that slapped like a line of wet washing.

"Don't be demented. D'you suppose they'd hear you any farther than ten yards, the way the wind's howling in the trees? And if they did, d'you suppose they'd take any notice, now they have their freedom?"

Lindsey had waded a few steps through the heather to a pine tree that towered darkly above the limits of her sight, and now she leaned herself wearily against its twisted trunk.

"Chalice might. He nearly always answers when I call him in the field."

There was no need to raise her voice much now; the wind threw it at Dion with the rain.

"That colt! He's at the root of all the trouble. If he hadn't started breaking out, the heifers wouldn't either. He taught them, and now nothing keeps them in. They even break their hobbles; what can anyone do? And if Duchess and the ponies hadn't been by themselves in Hanger field they'd all have got out, too."

The anger in Dion's voice made it loud enough to carry against the watery gusts, as he stood with his face to the weather.

Lindsey waited for him to finish before she shouted again to the colt, his name streaming down the dark wind in little beats like pulses; but if there was an answer she and Dion didn't hear it. They only heard the wind in the pine trees, like distant breakers crashing; and, though the whole wide jungle of the Punch Bowl plunged steeply all around them, they only saw the small disc of whipping heather and the silver slivers of the rain in Dion's torchlight.

"Coming?" he said, turning northwards, his raincoat clinging down the back of him like an extra skin and flapping round his knees.

"Oh, well——"

Lindsey hesitated, teetering in her mind. Someone must go on looking. Anything could happen to the colt before the morning. But the Punch Bowl was a fearful place in the blackness of a night of storm like this, and for someone alone it might be dangerous and bristling with horror. Her feet were heavy with weariness from trudging through the rough heather; the trees leaned down as she stood there, and there was a groaning in their branches. Dion began to move into the darkness towards the track, his doubled halter rope making snaky shadows at his feet.

"Wait!"

She was stumbling after him, her own torch bobbing. He turned and watched her coming, like a figure out of focus, then tramped along beside her with the wind like hands pushing them.

Reaching the stony track, they shone their torches low and wide upon it, looking for the least sign of colt and heifers. Dion stopped to scrape a wide dark patch with the toe of his boot.

"Might have been a cow-pat, but no one could say how old, or even if it ever was one, in all this rain."

Lindsey peered closely at the track all round the mark.

"Hoof-prints wouldn't last either. It really isn't much use looking for anything at all, except the animals themselves."

They went on, shoulders hunched up to help protect their necks from slashing rain squalls. The sky was only a half-shade lighter than the earth, and their torches now were wearing dim and flickery with long use. Lindsey hoarded the power of hers by switching off and sharing Dion's whenever possible; he needed his, of course, because of the nuisance of his eyes. He thought about this now, as they pushed on in the darkness. Other people wore spectacles of course, and in time became quite used to them; hardly noticing them, in fact, and doing such crazy things as looking around for them when they were really bang in place all the time. He supposed he would get used to wearing them too, some day, and he did have the great hopeful future to look forward to, when he might, the oculist had said, be able to do without them altogether. Now that the wind and rain were behind him he would try wearing them again; it was only when the rain ran down the lenses that they really were impossible.

They were only about a mile from home now. He was sorry he had been so crusty with old Lin, but where was the sense in floundering blindly around this desolate country any longer, when, for all they knew, the animals might be far in another direction, such as the deep wild valley, or down the hilly lane towards the village. Goodness knew, he wanted to find them quite as much as Lindsey did; more, probably, because of having bred and reared the heifers, whereas she really only cared about the colt; but they might just as well have tried looking for a button in a clover field. Besides, Lindsey wasn't yet fourteen, and as it was term-time she should have been in bed by half-past eight. He hadn't a watch (Andrea, the eldest, was the only Thornton child who had, and she was away at boarding school), but he supposed it must be quite that time already.

Lindsey was saying nothing, because she was saving her breath for calling the colt, and then straining her ears for any possible reply. Sometimes she half thought she heard the odd imperious high whinny that Chalice used to answer her, but there were so many strange noises in the whirling darkness of the Punch Bowl; it was difficult to be sure about any of the creaks and cracks, the howling and the moaning, and the shrill sad whining of the storm. Mostly, she thought, one's impressions were only of sound and touch, for so little could be seen. Their small private world of torchlight made the outer spaces even darker than they would have been without it, but in this stony, precipitous country, it would be madness to move without a light. There was, too, the sense of smell. All the smells were wet ones on this night; wet peaty earth, wet heather a little like wood smoke; wet bracken, dankly horrid; and wet pines. But sight . . . One could almost have done without it, except for guiding the tired, regular swing of shining wellingtons inside the small boundary of torchlight. She stared out again, beyond it, to the darkness—still calling.

"Chalice! Come colt, come colt!"

Soon they would be up on Highcomb Bottom and nearing the southernmost fields of Punchbowl Farm. It seemed silly to say "up" of a place called something Bottom, but the fact was that the Devil's Punch Bowl was a good deal lower still. It was just the same calling one of their own highest fields Lower Six Acres, because Upper Six Acres was even higher. She was looking out intently for the dark shapes against the sky that meant the group of pines where Highcomb Bottom started. There was a sort of floating white thing far away in the bracken that the faint fringes of her torchlight had found when she had flashed it in a wide half-circle just ahead of her. It was, perhaps, a bit of cloth hooked in a bramble—a piece of someone's shirt; or probably a strip of paper still surviving from early autumn trippers with their picnics. It was not the heifers, for they were both fawn with black points; and not the colt, for he

11

was the richest chestnut. The white thing swung low in the wind. It moved out of sight, then back into view again.

Lindsey touched a hand on Dion's shoulder.

"What's that?"

She pointed a wet, gloved hand, the halter hanging from it.

"What's what?"

"Can't you see it? Paper or cotton or something: moving a bit."

"No."

"Oh, sorry—I forgot."

She was miserable at forgetting so often about his eyes; it must only make things worse to keep drawing attention to the things he couldn't see. She called the colt again, loud and despairingly.

The white thing suddenly moved differently, so differently that Lindsey stopped and grabbed her brother by the elbow.

"Dion, it *lifted*! It lifted right up above the bracken!"

With the clarity of inspiration, Lindsey remembered Chalice's white blaze. It was more than a blaze, it was almost a white face; white from his broad brow right down to his pink and white striped muzzle.

"It's him! It's his white blaze; and the heifers will be with him! He swung his head up when he heard me calling."

How utterly crazy of her not to have remembered about his blaze until this minute! And now there was no doubt, for, as they hurried nearer, the doubled power from both their torches was lighting up the ruby-red eyes above the blaze—above it and beside it, for the heifers certainly were there with Chalice. Six glowing dark-red jewels hung suspended in the darkness, two higher than the others; and, unmistakable now in its nearness, came the clarion high-descending shiver of the colt's reply.

Lindsey, who could have cried from sheer relief and happiness, was blundering in her hurry through the heather; but Dion caught her arm.

"Steady, now! You'll scare them half across to Hind-head. Your torch is in their faces. Now, which one are we trying for first?"

Torch lowered, eyebrows drawn down in nervous

12

impatience as she slackened her pace, Lindsey answered, "Chalice, of course! He always lets me catch him."

"Don't be so sure. He may not know you for certain in the dark, and don't forget he's got his freedom now."

The six burning eyes still hung like planets in the night, and all round Dion's and Lindsey's feet there seemed to reach wet hands with fingers crooked to catch an ankle. This was because their eyes were on those other eyes, and the ground that stretched between them was untracked and thick with tangled scrub.

All the time Lindsey was talking to the colt. She hardly knew what she was saying. Mostly it was the rather silly, absurd kind of things one does say to very young creatures; but what really mattered to the colt was that it was Lindsey's voice saying them; and he recognised it (for the place and the night were both wild), even though it was a little unlike itself because of high excitement, nervousness and exhaustion.

A sudden crashing and crackling of woody heather stems was the scared leaping aside of the heifers as Dion and Lindsey came nearer. For one strained moment it seemed as if Chalice would go, too; his head in the fringe of the torchlight was up and turned away towards the two black blurs that were the heifers, yards away towards the valley. Then, with the distinctive voice he always used for close-up conversation—a low guttural whicker that was partly a snort—the colt took a wary step forwards, half sideways, eyes everywhere in the darkness. Lindsey went to meet him with all her nerves prickling, one hand delving damply in her pocket past the torch she had shoved there for the dairy-nuts the colt could never resist, and the other holding the sodden halter well behind her back from force of habit though the night was dark enough to hide a herd of elephants.

Dion's was the only light now, and they couldn't do without that. He was keeping it well lowered, and the colt could not be minding it for he took another step forward. Lindsey took two, and then—the racing relief of it—his small muzzle (all pink and white and richly whiskered) was pushing softly into her gloved hand, taking dairy-nuts with

13

quick prehensile lips. Lindsey's other hand came gently round from her back; it passed over the bushy, half-erect tousle of the mane, dropping the rope of the halter carefully, so carefully, down the far side of the colt's outstretched neck, till the hand that held the nuts could reach it when the last morsel had gone. Suddenly, the last fragment *had* gone; Chalice was blowing and snuffling, the halter rope was dangled nearer, and the hand beneath the exploring muzzle moved and closed its fingers. A little jerk upwards and sideways was the colt's reaction to knowing he was caught, but it didn't really mean anything as he had known what Lindsey was up to all the time. He was used to being caught, and he knew it always meant some small nice thing, such as a bowl of crushed oats, or being brushed beneath the throat where it felt all comfortable and dreamy; or even, perhaps (he hoped) being taken to his mother, who was after all the only thing he ever wandered for; but these last few days he never seemed to find her, for she was not in any of her usual places, and he missed her very much.

Lindsey's held breath went out with a sudden gust. Her whole body relaxed, the tension going from it like the air from a burst balloon.

"Oh, well *caught!*" said Dion fervently, just as if they were at a cricket match and the weather fair and sunny. "We needn't bother about the heifers now, I think; they're pretty sure to follow."

"Yes, I expect they will," said Lindsey, pulling the halter properly into place; but she knew she couldn't really care half so much about the heifers now she knew that Chalice couldn't in any circumstances be found lying with broken legs upon the Portsmouth road before morning.

"We'll shut him up for the night, to make sure," she said, holding out more rewarding tit-bits to the colt as she stumbled beside him to the track.

"He'll kick the door and neigh and wake up everybody."

"It can't be helped," said Lindsey happily. "There are some worse things than being woken up in the night."

Later on, splashing down the last bit of the lane towards the farm, Dion said, pausing to listen over his shoulder, "They're still coming. I can hear their hoofs on the stones."

14

"Oh, good," said Lindsey vaguely. Then, "I was just thinking—if ever I wanted to ride Chalice very secretly, one dark night when he is older—I'd have to paint his white blaze over. It shows up much more than you'd think."

CHAPTER TWO

A Problem Apiece

DION threw open the back door of Punchbowl Farmhouse and at once he and Lindsey were engulfed in the old warm atmosphere of comfort, light, security and family friendliness. No matter that they were both a little in disgrace because of the lateness of the hour and the wetness of their clothing; nothing could dim the glory of the farmhouse kitchen, and the magic of being inside the circle of the family, to whom this kitchen was the hub and heart of the house.

"Here you are at last! Dear me, wet right through," said their mother, coming across the kitchen, anxiously fussing, helping Lindsey's numbed fingers with the buttons of her raincoat.

"Never mind that, Mother, we've caught them!" said Lindsey, blinking and glowing in the mellowness of lamplight.

"Caught pneumonia, I should think; how *could* you keep her out so late, Dion? And you, too—just when you're supposed to be resting more."

Dion knew what she meant. That was part of the cure for his eye disorder, rest. As if anyone could, with school all day and homework in the evening, and so much to do on the farm that no day, ever, was long enough. It was much worse now, because one of the first things to go in this sudden family economy drive had been the farm man, Holleybone, who instead of coming every day as usual, now came only on Tuesdays and Thursdays, with extra days in very busy periods such as ploughing and haying and harvest.

"I'm not particularly tired. Hungry, though. What's that glorious smell?"

"Soup—but not till you've rubbed down and changed, and Lindsey's bathed. You ought both to bath really, but it's so late . . . Your raincoat, too, Dion. I'll hang them both in the boiler-room. Oh, and your wellingtons—they're as wet inside as out—I'll turn them upside-down."

Lindsey was dragging hers off, toe against heel. They were damply stuck and resistant, and her feet longed to be rid of them. She leaned back against the wall beneath the row of bridles hanging by the door, half-heartedly tugging at the boots, giving more of her mind to the weary contentment of being home again, being fussed by someone who now took all responsibility from her. She never tired of the sudden first impact of the kitchen on coming in from darkness and bad weather. It was a wide, low room, in which the nobleness of the great arched inglenook was the crowning beauty; but among the dark rafters were the shadows and pure whiteness that made the ceiling the only thinkable place for hanging up the cow-bells, the brass-handled cream skimmer, the shining milking bucket and the lanterns.

Looking at the cow-bells as her last boot slowly yielded, Lindsey suddenly said, "I say, I've got an idea——"

"Not now, darling," said her mother, catching up the boot almost before it was off. "Just *look* at the time! Straight up, this minute, and into the bath; Peter's been in bed nearly two hours. Oh—and throw Dion's bath towel down while you're there, will you? Don't be long now, and have the water as hot as you can bear it. And Dion, get into the inglenook till I bring you your towel."

"Don't forget to remind me, Dion," said Lindsey over her shoulder, padding in her wet socks across the floor, "to explain my idea when I come down."

Her footprints were Man-Friday marks upon the dark red tiles.

"Lindsey——" began her mother from the boiler-room.

"All right, Mother, I'm just going."

She hadn't heard Peter padding downstairs in his bare feet and pyjamas, but suddenly he was there, dancing on the cold tiles that felt like metal to his feet.

"Did you get them? Gosh! is that really the time? I

17

say, Dion, your hair's so wet it looks just like a skull-cap."

"You jolly well will catch it when Mother sees you," said Dion, drying his wet face on the roller towel on the door.

"You might tell a fellow! And after I've kept awake all this time."

"All caught," said Lindsey, "and all in. I hope you've left the bath clean?"

"*Peter!*" His mother appeared from the cavern of the boiler-room doorway. "Go back to bed *at once!* And Lindsey, if you don't go up this minute there won't be any soup."

"I say!" said Peter, rubbing one bare foot upon the other warm knee. "Soup. Couldn't I have some, too? I'm simply famished."

"Go back to *bed*, Peter! You had your supper hours ago."

"I know, that's why I'm famished."

"Oh, come on, Peter! Don't argue," said Lindsey, disappearing.

"Oh, well—it seems an awful shame! Just when I could've enjoyed it." But Peter disappeared, too.

At the inglenook Dion bent his head under the ten-foot span of delicately-arched brick, sat heavily in the wheel-backed arm-chair in the chimney corner and began to peel off his sodden socks. On the warm top of the Aga cooker, beside the covered pan of soup, two Siamese cats were folded neatly down with front paws tucked in sideways like the bluff bows of a barge. One, his mother's cat Vashti, was seal-pointed, with heavy contrasts between dark brown and cream, looking as if someone had swung her round and round till all the colour had run to her extremities; the other, Lindsey's half-grown kitten Freyni, was a blue-point, grey and silver like the tufts of pussy-willow. They regarded him with inscrutable blue eyes as he hung his socks over the chair arm, rubbed his glasses on his sleeve and then began peeling off his pullover.

"I'll get your pyjamas and dressing-gown," said his mother, bringing him his towel. She picked up the wet socks and hung them in the rack that was hidden high above the Aga. "I do hope," she added, half to herself, "that Peter wasn't really hungry. I shouldn't like to think that. But you know what he is. And at this time of night."

Dion had stripped to his vest and pants and was towelling his legs.

"I shouldn't think so. He just heard someone say 'soup'."

"Oh, well, I hope you're right." His mother sighed doubtfully. "Keep rubbing till I get your things, then we can have the soup in the sitting-room; there's a wonderful fire in there, and your father's got it all to himself at present, finishing the drawings for the angling book."

"I say," said Peter the next morning, "it just jolly well is a good thing it's Saturday. I did all my homework last night, but I don't suppose you and Dion touched yours."

They were feeding and bedding down the two heifers, Midnight and Whinberry, in the old square calf box while Dion was milking in the cowshed adjoining.

Lindsey said, "You wouldn't have, if you'd come out with us and helped find the heifers and Chalice; you wouldn't have done any of it."

She lifted the forkload of hay she was carrying and dropped it into the hay-rack, the metal tines of her fork catching against the wooden rail with a musical springy noise.

Peter was scattering dried bracken bedding, brown and crisp and frondy.

"What a *rotten* thing to say!" he exploded. "And when I did ask Mother if I could."

The heifers, wishing to be let out in the early autumn sunshine, bucketed around them, their hoofs rustling dryly in the bracken.

"No rottener than what you said about homework."

"You know what I think," said Peter, changing the subject, and noticing by the deeper, frothier noise in the cowshed that Dion must be getting near the end of the milking. "What I think is that, if we had Moonstone back, Chalice would give up wandering to look for her, and then the heifers wouldn't keep breaking out too, and everything would be all right again."

"Oh, do shut up, Peter!" said Lindsey, as she paused to

19

pick haystems from her jersey. "People can't just have things back, like that, when they've sold them. It's just like very small children thinking they can take things back again whenever they feel like it, once they've given them away. Besides, you only make everyone miserable by keeping on harping about Moonstone. D'you think Mother and Father would have sold her, or Clover either, unless they couldn't afford to keep them? And if two of them *had* to go, wouldn't you rather it was the one too small and the one too lame for us to ride, than Nanti or Sula, which we can? Now, jolly well don't say any more about it. We're all as sick as you are over losing them; at least they've gone to a much better home than we could ever have given them—well, anyway, as good."

There was a clanking of a bucket handle in the cowshed, which meant that Dion had finished milking, and a moment later he was looking over the half-door into the calf box.

"Scrapping again?"

"What d'you mean, 'again'? We haven't scrapped for days," said Peter indignantly. "And did you know that Midnight has a sore place on her foreleg?"

"She has?" Dion was concerned at once. "That must be where we tried hobbling her. Half a minute while I hang the milk bucket up—we don't want all the cats and geese to find it—and I'll come and look."

"You hang on to her," said Peter to Lindsey, "and I'll show him the place. I may be a boy, but you're older than me, and far heavier."

"I wish you wouldn't keep talking as if I were the Fat Lady or something! There's nothing to grab her with; pass me that halter hanging on the nail—thanks!"

Lindsey caught the young heifer as she skirmished past, neatly looping the rope round her neck. Whinberry, the other one, stopped still with straddled legs, goggling from a corner; but Midnight, now she was roped, was suddenly friendly and quiet, lowering her head when Lindsey scratched between her stumpy horns.

"There it is," said Peter as Dion came in. "It does look rather raw-ish."

"That was the hobble all right," said Dion, bending to

20

examine it. "She must have put some pressure on it before she broke it. What about Whinberry?"

Lindsey screwed round to look at the other heifer, and Dion and Peter glanced up. Whinberry snorted and backed a step into the corner.

"Nothing wrong with her," said Dion in a relieved voice. "We couldn't see very much last night, of course. I'll put some of that carbolised oil on; pass it, will you, Pete—it's

"That was the hobble all right," said Dion

up there on the beam above the door—yellow bottle— thanks!"

Lindsey gave a sudden agonised yelp and shoved Midnight sideways.

"They always step on your feet—when there's all this straw around to step on instead."

"I know," said Dion, tipping oil on to his fingers. "Like with grapefruits; they never fail to get your eye. Wonderful aim, really, when you think of the scope there is for them. Stop hopping about; you're making Midnight fidget."

"I'll tell you what," said Lindsey, suddenly enthusiastic. "Speaking of hobbling has reminded me of the idea I had

21

last night: the one you were going to remind me about after my bath, but you didn't. It was the cow-bells made me think of it. Why don't we bell the heifers, the way they do in Switzerland? After all, the bells may be ornamental and all that, but they must have been meant for use."

Peter turned round from looking over the door into the farmyard.

"That won't stop them breaking out, chump!"

"Chump yourself—honestly, Peter, sometimes you're absolutely *simple!* What the bells are for is so that we can *hear* them when they break out, and not just wander about blindly, never knowing whether they're ten yards away or ten miles. Think if we hadn't seen Chalice's blaze last night! We'd have passed within a stone's throw of the lot of them, and gone home never knowing it."

"I still think," persisted Peter, "that what we want is to stop them *getting* out."

Dion straightened up, corking the bottle. "I think it's worth trying. Quite a good idea, in fact. Of course, we want to stop them getting out, but till we can do that we want to be able to find them when they do get out."

"How are you going to fix them on?" asked Peter. "Mother won't be awfully pleased if the heifers lose them in the Punch Bowl."

"Never mind that now," said Dion, watching Midnight buck-jump as Lindsey slipped the halter from her neck. "We can think that out later. I've got to take the milk up to the house; it doesn't strain properly when it's cold. That leg'll be all right now," he added, opening the door. "Jolly good thing it isn't the fly season, or it'd be a different tale."

Peter and Lindsey collected their pitchforks and followed him.

"Wonder what time it is?" speculated Peter. "Should you think time enough to do my rabbit and hamsters before breakfast?"

"Gosh, I should hope so! I've still got to do the hens and geese and a feed for Chalice, myself."

Racing across the farmyard to the workshop for the hen food, Lindsey paused a moment at Barn Field gate to stare in wonder at the transformation of the deep valley-shaped field in early-morning sunlight. The grass was so thickly studded with the drops of the night's heavy rain, and the sun low behind it, shining through it, that the whole field was silvered over in sweeping drifts. As if millions of the smallest, whitest flowers had blown there, Lindsey thought suddenly—but as suddenly remembered hen food and ran on.

At breakfast everyone was rather abstracted. This morning seemed to have a problem apiece for the Thorntons. It started with Peter rushing in and saying his rabbit, Mr. Muncher, had got out and he simply must find him before he had a bite of breakfast; and, though his mother began by saying, "But, Peter——" he affected not to hear and rushed away again.

Then Mr. Thornton wandered into the kitchen, where breakfast was almost ready and the coffee smelt quite wonderful, and said he couldn't remember what a dace looked like; none of his reference books had any photographs of one, and if he couldn't find out soon he wouldn't be able to do the drawings for the angling book at all, and then they'd probably have to sell the heifers too, or go into the workhouse.

Mrs. Thornton had her own immediate troubles enough, including the mess the moles were making of the north lawn, and how on earth to make the sitting-room loose covers do another year, despite the Siamese cats, but she told him not to be so pessimistic, it was bad for the children, and she suggested Godalming Library, but said that meanwhile the toast was nearly ready, and she could never think why it was always so impossible to collect all the Thorntons together at the same time for the same meal.

Lindsey, who was making the toast on the Aga hotplate, forgot it utterly and let it gallop itself to ruin, because she suddenly caught sight of her own Siamese, Freyni, limping into the kitchen, with one hind leg noticeably swollen.

"But, Mother, *look* at her! Freyni, Freyni darling, what *have* you done to yourself? Oh, Mother! do you suppose it's an adder bite?"

23

Lindsey had picked up her kitten and was touching along the swollen leg with sensitive, searching fingertips.

Mrs. Thornton rescued the toast and dropped it regretfully into the chickens' saucepan on the small table by the door.

"I shouldn't think so, darling—in October. Wouldn't they mostly be hibernating? Let me have a look at her."

"What, no toast?" said Mr. Thornton, looking at the empty toast-rack. "Here, pass me the loaf and I'll make some myself." His voice had the resigned and slightly irate tone of one with whom Fate has dealt badly.

"There's porridge in the bottom oven, dear," said Mrs. Thornton, "only taste it first—I think I forgot to put the salt in it. There isn't any sign of a bite, Lindsey, the leg seems just the same all the way up . . . Dion, could you get me the Dettol out of the first-aid cupboard, please? I think we'd better dab a little on wherever it's swollen."

"Oh—all right," said Dion in a descending voice. "I was just trying to work out how to hang the cow-bells. I was thinking, have we any spare stirrup-leathers? We ought to have now we've got less ponies, and if we have, I thought they'd cut down nicely to make collars for the heifers——"

"I simply don't know what you're talking about, dear," said his mother, "but would you mind going to get the Dettol now? Freyni's started struggling, and the coffee's going cold, and we're already late for breakfast."

"And the toast's cremated," added Mr. Thornton sadly. "By the way, Dion, do you know what a dace looks like, by any chance?"

"I don't even know what a dace is," said Dion frankly, moving slowly to the door. "But, Dad, d'you think wire around leather collars would rub the heifers' necks?"

"Dion——" began Mrs. Thornton, and Lindsey said, "If it was you who was trying to hold an injured kitten without hurting it, you'd jolly well see that people *ran*."

"All right, all right, I'm going," said Dion. "Anyone'd think there'd been an air-raid."

There was a sudden loud hissing noise, followed by an appalling smell.

"That's the milk for the coffee, I suppose," said Mr.

Thornton bitterly. "How like it, just on this morning! I expect the table will collapse next and pitch the lot on the floor."

Mrs. Thornton left Lindsey and Freyni and rushed to the inglenook to the rescue of the milk.

"Oh dear! Coffee boiled is coffee spoiled. Not that it was the coffee," she added accurately, "but it amounts to the same thing with milk that's meant for it."

"It couldn't be a wasp sting now either, I suppose," Lindsey was speculating. "Except perhaps a queen wasp. Do hurry, Mother! Vashti's all under my feet now, and Freyni's just like a greased pig to hold. I say, don't you think we ought to phone for the vet?"

"No, I don't think so," answered Mrs. Thornton, advancing with the Dettol which Dion had brought "Not until we see if it's going down, anyway. Let's give the treatment a chance. Now, just hold her quite still if you can."

"She *was* quite still, five minutes ago."

"Shall I put on some more milk for the coffee?" asked Dion. "And would you like me to give a shout for Peter,"

"Yes, do, dear, thank you—the coffee milk and Peter. And tell him he must leave the rabbit alone and come at once, or there won't be any breakfast for him. There, Lindsey, I think Freyni'll be all right now, so for goodness' sake let's have breakfast, before anything else happens."

"It's happening now," said Dion, coming in from calling Peter. "Postman. I'd know his long step and soft whistling anywhere. Any letters for him to take back?"

But Mrs. Thornton had not heard.

"George!" she said to her husband despairingly. "Do you know that's the grocer's bill you're drawing fish all over? I had it all ready for paying him!"

CHAPTER THREE

October Morning

THE postman (having said it was a lovely day, such a change from yesterday, and did they know Peter's rabbit was out in the Old Orchard?) handed in the papers and a letter from Andrea to her mother. Mrs. Thornton settled down to read the letter, with complete absorption, though it was quite probably full of news about people wholly unknown to her, and with nothing at all about Andrea herself, except possibly her poor opinion of the geography mistress, or more about her regret at having won a scholarship to a famous boarding-school while the other Thorntons blissfully continued at their day school over Hindhead Common.

By the time Mrs. Thornton had finished this letter, and read it again more carefully in case there might be something she had missed, Peter had bolted his hasty breakfast and rushed out again to resume the stalking of his rabbit; Mr. Thornton had reached his second cup of coffee and was drawing imaginary dace round the edges of the *Daily Telegraph* while at the same time casting an eye over the more important headlines, and Dion and Lindsey were doing a sort of cross-talk act about Freyni and the belling of the heifers.

"We'd better rub in some neat's-foot oil," said Dion, "against the weather."

"Are you sure it would do her any good?" asked Lindsey, with vague anxiety. "We did her with that antiseptic stuff you know, just before we sat down. What I really think we ought to do is ring the vet, and tell him it's jolly urgent."

"The vet?" Dion's mug of coffee wavered in the air before him. "For that little place she rubbed on her leg, d'you mean? What *are* you talking about? That's only a surface graze from her hobbles, you ass; it's the collars I mean—

26

oiling them to make them stand the weather. Hey! That's my piece of toast!"

"Oh, is it? Sorry, I didn't know I'd had one."

Mrs. Thornton folded Andrea's letter and pushed it back inside its envelope.

"What *is* all this about, you absurd people?" She looked at them with mild affection, thinking how nice it was that Lindsey's hair was really noticeably growing,* after the dreadful time when she had cut it in the summer, and how Dion's jacket would be positively through at the elbows if she didn't somehow get round to patching it with those bits of leather she'd been saving since she'd tried to make herself a pair of brown moccasins.

"Well, I was talking about Freyni, of course," said Lindsey, screwing round in her chair to see if the swollen leg might possibly be looking any better.

"The heifers," said Dion at the same time. "About belling them, Mother."

"What, with my cow-bells?"

"Well, it does seem the most sensible thing," said Dion reasonably. "I mean, that's what they're for, isn't it?"

"It isn't what *my* cow-bells are meant for," his mother pointed out with equal reasonableness. "They're meant to hang in the rafters and look decorative. At least, that's what I meant them for when I bought them."

"It can't hurt cow-bells to be worn by cows," said Dion.

"No, but it could hurt them to be lost by cows."

Mr. Thornton looked up suddenly for a moment, pencil in hand, and said, "Who lost the cows?" but plainly took no interest in the conversation so nobody bothered to explain.

Dion began to describe how he planned to hang the cow-bells, with strong wire rings on spare stirrup-leather collars, and Mrs. Thornton was just saying how she might be more easy in her mind about the matter if they had proper brass D-rings fitted, when Peter suddenly tore into the kitchen again.

"I say, can't anybody help me with Mr. Muncher? It's absolutely no use at all, by myself. I keep getting practically

*Told in *Spirit of Punchbowl Farm.*

right up to him, and he hops clean out of reach. It's been going on for hours."

"Ten minutes," said Mr. Thornton, glancing up, his forehead crinkled because he wasn't looking up quite high enough, his mind still being on the drawings on the paper.

"Well it seems like hours. Can *you* give me a hand, Dad? I know Dion and Lindsey won't."

"Oh, all right, if you know we won't there isn't any use your asking us," said Lindsey, twisting herself off her chair and pushing it back under the big table.

"Don't forget the breakfast dishes and your room, darling," her mother reminded her. "Particularly your room; when I glanced in there this morning it looked as if there'd been an earthquake. Music sheets all over the bed and clothes on the floor—two handkerchiefs on the window-ledge and a saddle in the corner——"

"All right," Lindsey sighed, slowing down a little through discouragement as she began to clear the table.

"Can't you give me just five minutes, Lin?" asked Peter hopefully, kicking the wall with his heel.

"You said yourself it was no use asking us." Lindsey tipped the bread board, scraping the crumbs on to the tablecloth.

"You asked me, but didn't wait for an answer, old chap," said Mr. Thornton, folding the paper finally as he left the breakfast table. "And please stop kicking the wall; that plaster's so old it might fall down even if you just looked at it too hard."

"Oh sorry, Dad—I say, thanks awfully, Dad! "

"I didn't say I was coming."

"Oh, Dad! "

"Oh, all right then; but why we keep any animals at all on this place is more than I can understand. We take it as a ruined old house in the country, with a lot of derelict land we didn't really want at all, and the next thing is Dion's up to the neck in farming it, despite all I said and the fact that he's still at school and would be much better off playing football in his spare time—to say nothing of what the over-strain has already done to his eyesight."

Dion made no effort at all to answer this; it had all been

28

said so often; but his mother said placidly, "Don't be silly, George dear! You know perfectly well you bought the first cow yourself, and everything else started from that. You should really be thankful Dion does do all he does, as I can't imagine what would happen if he left it all to you. And we can't be at all sure about what caused Dion's eye disorder. I dare say, myself, it had a lot to do with reading in bed by torchlight, as I said at the time."

She opened a wide, low door, painted cream colour, and slowly disappeared from sight as she went sideways down the steep stairs into the cellar with a bowl of thick cream in her hands.

Mr. Thornton sat down by the door to put his wellingtons on, making no answer as Mrs. Thornton could not now have heard him, even if he had been able to think of one. Peter hopped impatiently about from one foot to the other, looking over the empty plates on the breakfast table to see if they might contain anything that would be likely to tempt an escaped rabbit.

Dion rushed upstairs to make his bed and tidy his room, for Mrs. Thornton saw no reason why boys, as well as girls, should not take their share of the work in a servantless household.

Lindsey began to pick up speed with the table clearing, putting down any plates and dishes that the cats might like to lick (and getting into trouble with her father who nearly trod on one as he went out after Peter), stacking everything else on the draining board and window-ledge and anywhere she could find room. She was too pre-occupied and worried about Freyni to play her usual washing-up game (which was rather like patience, except that you musn't move anything once you've put it in the drying rack), but spent her time instead trying to think out a little verse she had been brewing somewhere in the back of her mind, about Chalice's repeated escapes. The verse, as verses do, refused to come the way she had expected it, and instead of being a rousing Song of Escape began to grow into a wistful Song of Seeking. The first two lines, coming quite of their own accord into Lindsey's mind, even had a plaintive tune which sang itself to the words:

*O come, my little chestnut colt,
Do not wander in the night . . .*

You don't have to rhyme the first line with anything, Lindsey told herself, so the third line is always the easiest. In a few more minutes, before she had got to the bacon plates even, it had arrived:

Where the bracken and the gorse . . .

But the dishes were all finished, her bed made and her room almost tidy enough to pass a hurried inspection before she had worked her way far enough through the alphabet for the rhyme "sight", which almost at once rushed itself into the final line:

Hide you from my (something) *sight.*

What sight? Lindsey asked herself, not even consciously worrying about Freyni because of the absorbing interest of chasing the elusive right word. It must be two syllables, she frowned, pushing her old grey jersey out of sight beneath her bed and at the same time being aware of the usual prick of conscience for scamping the tidying; but her bottom drawer was already full to explosion point (mostly, she knew, with things that shouldn't be in it, such as scraps for making stocking people and horses, as well as her recorder, wrapped round with an old shantung handkerchief). And her mother would be the first person to mention it if jerseys were bundled into the other drawer with the underclothes and pyjamas and things.

The thought of her recorder brought a sudden happy idea. Perhaps if she got it out and played the tune she had thought of, it might help her to think of the elusive word. Playing the recorder was fun now she wasn't a fumbling learner any more; though she was still a learner of course, for one could go on learning something about everything for all one's life, but she wasn't a fumbling learner any more. Her fingers knew where the holes were now, without her having to tell them every time, and her old troubles with B-flat and Bottom-C were happily a thing of the past.

Lindsey pulled the drawer open and thrust a hand down between the woollens and the drawer front. Her fingers closed round the curiously rough-smooth surface of the

30

shantung handkerchief. Sitting on the edge of her bed, looking out of the small casement window to the old Well House and the great triple yew tree high behind it, she played the tune over, cautiously, once or twice, and the word slipped itself in; "shadowed".

Hide you from my shadowed sight.

It was probably not exactly what she had meant, but it was near enough. It carried out the theme of night and sadness, and it had two syllables. She began to play it all over again, altering a note or two here and there, and she would probably have gone on playing for almost the rest of the morning if people would only have left her in peace to do it. But first it was Peter, barging in noisily, all out of breath and with his hair stuck out at windy angles, asking if she knew where his butterfly-net was, as she had borrowed it for frogspawn in the spring and it was just the thing for catching Mr. Muncher.

By the time Lindsey had found the net (which was in the stable behind the corn-bin) and cleaned it to the degree Peter thought would be required by a decently brought-up rabbit, and then lost a further few minutes by dallying pleasantly with Chalice in the cobwebby shadows of his loose-box, it was almost too late to recapture the mood of the music any more.

Chalice's box was really a farm-horse's stall, fenced off with two poles, and he was annoyed at being kept in it all by himself when Nanti and the grey pony Sula and Duchess the cow were all out in the glory of the mellow October morning. So Lindsey stayed another few minutes, teaching the colt to have his feet picked up and rapped, so that he wouldn't mind being shod when the time came. He was very good about this. In fact the only things he wasn't very good about were being led and keeping his teeth to himself. He had always been far too ready with his teeth, and when he was younger he had been excused on the grounds of teething troubles.

"He's only cutting his teeth, you know. It isn't really *biting*."

31

But now he nipped even harder and oftener it seemed, though only in play, because he hadn't any vice in him. However, it doesn't hurt any less when you know it's only meant in play, Lindsey thought, and she was particularly defenceless against nipping while she bent to lift a small white hoof and bang it with her knuckles or a stone.

After a bit she stopped doing this and patted Chalice's neck, noticing how his short mane was beginning to sag over from its baby erectness, like a fence that needs propping. He blew at her, with the sudden dreamy friendliness he could effect just after having nipped his hardest, flapping his pink-and-white lips on which the whiskers sprouted stiffly like the rays of a sun drawn by a very little child. Lindsey blew back, because he liked that and it made him shut his eyes. She was doing this when Peter reappeared with the butterfly-net.

"What *are* you doing? I say, this net was no earthly good. He jumped away from it every time, just the same as he did from my hands. And now Dad's gone in to draw his beastly fish and Mr. Muncher's gone into Hanger field. You don't think he'll go and join the wild ones, do you?"

"I shouldn't think so. Not with that piebald colouring. I mean, they wouldn't have him, would they?"

"Of course they would!" Peter began, scenting an insult to Mr. Muncher, but Lindsey had already changed the subject.

"You know what I was just thinking? D'you remember reading in that equitation book we had from the library about how you could always tell a horse's true colour by looking at his muzzle? Well, look at Chalice's! You didn't know we had a pink-and-white striped colt, did you!"

Peter giggled, twizzling the long handle of the net between his fingers.

"Don't do that, you ass! You'll frighten him—and besides, what about Exmoors? Mealy muzzles and brown ponies."

Peter propped the butterfly-net in the corner behind the corn bin.

"Dion asked me to tell you he wants you to help him with belling the heifers."

32

"Oh," said Lindsey doubtfully. "What, just like that? Not even saying please or anything?"

Peter hesitated a moment on the threshold, framed in yellow sunlight that seemed clearer and more golden in the rain-washed air.

"Well, he might have; does it matter? Anyway, he wants you to help."

"Of course it matters. There's no need to help anyone who doesn't even ask you decently; but when they do, well, you sort of have to, I suppose."

She was running the fingers of one hand down through the thick chestnut depths of Chalice's growing winter coat, making a pattern of parallel valleys plunging downwards.

"Don't be an ass," said Peter, grinning tolerantly. "You let him take advantage of you. What you ought to do is stand up to him—I do. Well, after all, he wouldn't help me catch old Muncher, you saw for yourself. And you know what Dion is; you've only got to stand around blowing your nose or something for half a minute and he's got you driving the tractor or mucking-out the cowshed. What I'm going to do is, leave Muncher for a bit to cool down, and catch Sula and ride through the Punch Bowl and round by Boundless Farm. I'll catch Nanti too if you'll come with me. . . . It's a marvellous morning," he added, seeing Lindsey waver.

She was wavering, but only for a minute. A lot of things can race round anyone's mind in less than a minute. In her minute Lindsey thought ecstatically of what it would be like to canter Nanti through the long woods by Boundless Farm—all copper-golden as they were in autumn foliage—of how Chalice's breaking-out was at the bottom of all the trouble with the heifers, and if she didn't do all she could to make up for it, Dion would surely set himself against the colt as he had always set himself against anything that threatened his farming activities. (There was the yew tree, the summer before; how nearly that had gone to the timber merchants after poisoning the heifer Dawn with its deadly twigs, Lindsey would never forget, just as she could never forget the trouble about the fallow deer before that.)* And

*Told in *Spirit of Punchbowl Farm* and *Punchbowl Midnight*.

33

B

if Chalice had to go, after all the losses they had sustained at Punchbowl Farm from animals poisoned, dead, or sold, it would be just too much—too much for any bearing.

"Coming?" asked Peter impatiently, one shoulder in table shadow and one in outside sunlight. "Oh, come on! You know you'll enjoy it."

"No," said Lindsey suddenly. "I think I'd better help Dion. I suppose he's in the cowshed?"

"Honestly, Lin, you're *hopeless!* All right, slog if you want to, I'm going."

Lindsey watched him snatch Sula's little head-collar from its peg and go swinging out through the doorway. With a small sign she gave the colt a farewell pat, climbed over the pole-barrier and went out, too.

Crossing the yard she saw Vashti hunting on the straw-stack—alone, with no snowy-coloured Freyni bouncing round and spoiling all the hunting. With a rush, the early-morning's worry about Freyni came tumbling back into her mind. How was the leg? Could it really have been an adder? And, if not, what was it? Would Freyni get better, or was she going to be another one in the sad procession of animals they had once owned?

Lindsey thought of the odd things that made up the sum of Freyni's delightfulness: her wayward independence, her adorable smugness, the way she had of smiling with half-shut eyes, and of chirruping with a purr-meaow sound when she came walking in; of her smoky-blue ears and tail which were all too short, and her figure which was too round, for Siamese standards, but which made her all the more special and loved in Lindsey's eyes.

Going into the cowshed, Lindsey thought that life on the whole was much fuller of heartache than it ever was of joy; but there was Dion in his dungarees, bending over a pair of dusty stirrup-leathers on the edge of Duchess's manger, and whatever sorrow was gnawing at your vitals there was always work to take your mind off it.

"Oh, there you are," he said, with a sudden wide smile that almost made up for any doubts about the message he had sent her. "Mother says we can if we get some proper D-rings as soon as someone goes to Godalming. Can you

34

go on punching these holes, about the same spaces I've been doing, while I get the wire rings twisted for the bells? And I was thinking: if we could find another leather we could make one for Chalice as well."

CHAPTER FOUR

"So Silently, So Cunningly . . ."

IN the gold of the afternoon Dion and Peter went up on the high rough fields with the little four-ten shotgun and a bundle of seasoned rabbit wires. In some ways, Dion would rather have had Lindsey with him, because she could be more depended on to keep quiet when he was coming up silently to gaps in hedges where rabbits might be out; but in other ways Peter was more satisfactory, for Lindsey never grew out of her squeamishness about killing anything whatever—even rabbits, which were the menace of the district—and that was a very great drawback to anyone living on a farm, where after all there was bound to be the Christmas goose, the old boiling fowl, and probably the bacon pig, as well as a rabbit or a pheasant from the fields and woods about the place.

Lindsey, however, had not been available on this afternoon, which was unlike her; she was usually the one person in the whole family that Dion could fairly count on to do almost anything for or with him. But just now she was bathing Freyni's leg in hot antiseptic water, and was quite firm about going on doing it, and after that taking Chalice for a walk because he had been kept in the stable all the night and morning. So it was just as well that Peter had not insisted on spending the rest of the day hunting Mr. Muncher, for, by himself, he wouldn't have been able to get round all the snares before milking time.

"I want to work round and come back through the top of Barn field, to make sure the heifers are still there," Dion was saying as they walked round the edge of Yew Tree field. His voice was pitched very low so that any rabbits on the corner of Lower Naps might not hear the sound of their approach along the track, below the overhanging hollies of the hedge.

"Did you know," said Peter, looking backwards, "that Vashti's following us?"

"Oh, darn! No!" Dion turned with swift annoyance to see the approaching dark triangle of Vashti's face showing up sharply against the whiteness of her front. "I did ask Lindsey not to let her out. Be a sport and take her back—and for Mike's sake tell Lindsey to see she doesn't get out this time. I'll get on with laying the first snare."

By the time Peter caught up again, Dion had crept to the corner of Lower Naps, fired at a running rabbit that was almost certainly out of range for his small gun and consequently missed it, and he was now bending to consider the place for the first snare, a rabbit run beneath the spreading holly hedge.

"I heard your shot! Any luck?"

"No. Too far away. Heard us coming, I expect."

Dion was rubbing his hands in the grass to take away their human smell.

"Lin says she didn't let Vashti out, and that she must have got out of a bedroom window," said Peter.

Dion grunted, giving his mind to the delicate adjustment of the snare. It looked a simple thing; a long copper wire with a running loop at one end and two stout strings at the other, but precision in the setting of it made all the difference that lies between a harmless piece of wire and a snare of deadly efficiency.

"Just ahead of where the rabbit's forefeet land," said Dion, half to himself. "That's the place, don't you think? Where it jumps that frond of bracken."

Crouching in the damp grass, Peter stared at the place, a little tunnel through the bottom of the hedge, about a rabbit's size, the dead leaves trodden here and there along it and, as Dion said, the flattened place showing where the bent frond of bracken had frequently been jumped. All along the bracken points were hung raindrops left from the night's heavy downpour, and the hedge smelt damp and jungly.

"Looks like it," said Peter. "Shall I knock in the peg?" He pulled one from his pocket. One end of it was sharpened to a point, and round the other a notched groove had been

37

cut. It had been made, with many others, on rainy summer evenings in the barn and left to season in the weather with the snares.

"Just here," Dion said, pointing a little to the side of the chosen landing-place.

With his heel Peter drove in the peg and Dion tied the strings of the snare firmly round the grooved top of it. Then from his pocket he pulled a thin setting-pin, weathered in the open outside the farmhouse with the wires and tethering-pegs so that the rabbits would not so easily see or smell them, and with it he carefully propped the noose above the rabbit run. Sitting back on his heels he studied the snare for a minute, checking height and distance. Four fingers' height above the ground the snare was to be, and the distance must be judged, not measured, for both the run and the noose would hold the scent of a boy's hand. Even a hand rubbed in earth was not to be trusted too freely.

The adjustment finally made to his satisfaction, he bent a spray of brown bracken over to hide the top of the tethering peg and stood up.

"Got plenty of wires and pegs?" he asked Peter, picking up his gun.

"About eight or nine."

"Good. If you'll go down to the broom thicket by the wood and put about four down there—there are lots of good runs—I'll go up to the birch coppice. I might get a shot in the corner of Lower Six Acres on the way, it's a good place; usually. Then we'll go straight on up the fields."

"Right, I'll come to the coppice when I've finished. I say, you don't suppose Vashti'll go after Mr. Muncher before morning, do you? After all, he is a rabbit."

"I shouldn't think so. She must know he's a sort of family one, by now, the same as the hens." Dion broke his gun at the breach, took out the empty cartridge and slipped a new one in. "Don't forget not to touch the wires or the runs, or to alter the look of the runs any more than you can help."

Peter nodded, moving quickly off along the scarlet-studded holly hedge, his dark green jersey almost lost against the sombre green of the holly leaves.

Dion turned up the field in the other direction, discovering at once the wretched fact that the sun, low in the south-west, was shining straight at the lenses of his glasses with a resulting glare that made accurate vision for shooting quite impossible. This, he thought glumly, was just his luck, for the corner of Lower Six Acres was the one place on the farm where, more than any other, the chances were that rabbits would be out and be in range of his four-ten. He paused a moment, watching Peter striding down to the broom thicket. On the quiet air he could hear the distant tinkle of the heifers' bells; on two notes they were, pure and sweet, like water in a brook, and they were reassuring, for they meant that the heifers could not be very far away —most probably just where they ought to be, in Barn field, in fact. He stretched out a hand to take a blackberry but, though plump and dark, it was horrid in the mouth. It was past their season, for in October, the country people said, "the Devil spat on them."

Walking on, it seemed to Dion that he might after all be able to get the better of the sun at the corner of Lower Six Acres if he tried shooting from the ground. At that level the high hedge would probably shade his glasses. It was still a pity though, because he was used to shooting only on his feet, and everyone does best with familiar methods. On the other hand, thought Dion, moving very silently now towards the corner, it's a good thing to try anything new when you can.

At the gap in the oak thicket dividing the fields, he dropped quietly on all fours, the gun still held carefully, uncocked, in the closed fist of his right hand. From now on he must be as silent as the dead. If a twig were snapped, or a stone set rolling, there would be a warning thud-thud of hind feet round the corner of the copse and the rabbits would be gone from the short range of his gun. With a bigger gun, now—say a twelve-bore—he would have double the range, and instead of being mainly a stalking job, shooting would really be shooting. There was one thing about starting on a four-ten, though, he remembered, as he

39

crept another two yards forward, picking every spot for hand or foot, Jim Faithful at Rockfield Farm next door had once said it was the finest training you could have for using bigger guns, for when you were a good shot with a four-ten you could be a crack shot with anything else.

Another yard forward, moving like a stoat with taut alertness, and he was almost through the little copse. Slowly, carefully, he cocked the hammer of the gun, trying by controlled effort to avoid the soft *click* as metal touched metal. But what he heard was not the expected metallic sound of the hammer; it was a distinct but muted Siamese chirrup. Quite close too—practically at his heels. Dion whipped his head round, eyebrows drawn down level with annoyance, and was staring into squinting sapphire eyes a yard away from his own brown ones. So, she had again foxed Lindsey, the devil take her! Signalling her away with a furious hand, he frowned with forbidding anger, but Vashti saw fit to notice neither hand nor frown. For so silently, so cunningly had she arrived here she would not now be turned back by mere anger. Her eyes, sloping and vivid, returned his glance intently, and with a silent flicker of dark lips she answered her defiance, knowing better than to utter at this moment. Looking at her in exasperated astonishment, Dion wondered what to do. She was crouched low to the ground, like a hunting leopard, watchful, making no movement except for the smallest quiver of her tail-tip. Plainly, she did not mean to leave him. By strategy she had escaped from the farmhouse, by cunning she had trailed him, and by sheer persistence she would stay now she had found him.

All right, you witch-cat you, said Dion to himself, not daring to speak aloud for fear the rabbits might yet be out and hear him (for Vashti had made little noise to frighten them), if you must come with me, you'll darned well make yourself useful. And one sound from you, he added, conveying the threat with eyes and gestures, and I'll conk you with the gun-stock.

A lift and swing of her black tail was all the reply the cat made to him, and when he turned and crept onwards she was creeping soundlessly behind him. He knew she was there, though not even a leaf-rustle advertised her movements.

Dion was right on the edge of the thicket now, but hidden from the corner of the field by a jutting promontory of green-brown bracken, still wet with rain and dew. The smell of it was a bitter tang in his nostrils, damp and pungent, and in the forest of its bare stalks the autumn leaves had drifted. He had been right about the sun; from his low position it was behind the tall westerly hedge. The broad shadow cast itself

What he heard, was a distinct but muted Siamese chirrup

clear beyond the place where the boy and the cat crouched motionless behind the bracken. It lay along the edge of the field like a dark green border on a great grass-green carpet, and, when Dion moved slowly, slowly, four inches farther onward, he saw in that border, with a sudden leap of excitement, the ears of four grazing rabbits. In the deep grass and clover ley of the field it was the ears that showed most clearly. In the near-distance and through spectacles they looked like tufts of bracken sticking up, but a watcher could soon see that the way they moved was not the way of bracken bobbing in the wind.

One quick glance told Dion that no rabbits were within the twenty-five yards' range of his gun. It was disappointing, after his careful stalking and the astonishing quietness of Vashti. She still made no sound, or visible movement, though she must have seen the rabbits hopping here and there in the clover. Drat them! thought Dion angrily, whatever you try to grow they eat it down. Corn spoilt, young fruit trees barked and ruined, the grazings bitten down and soured, roots gnawed. And there were such thousands and thousands of them—he longed to shift a foot that ached, but dared not, in case a rabbit should move nearer or come bounding from the undergrowth across the shadowy corner. No matter how well you kept the rabbits down on your own place, if you lived in a spot like this, right next to the Devil's Punch Bowl and the valley, they just rushed in from all the wild land and you were back again where you started.

While thinking these things, Dion had seen one pair of long ears slowly coming nearer. There was a short hop, a long bound, a nibble (at his clover ley) and then another hop, and the ears were definitely nearer. You never know, thought Dion, hoping urgently that Vashti would not spoil everything after all by sudden noise or movement. He would have liked to edge the stock of his gun a little nearer to his shoulder but dared not risk the rabbit's seeing him. He would just have to hope that he'd be quick enough, if and when the moment came. But the rabbit had stopped, turned right round and began to nibble a plant of clover. Now would have been a safe time to shift the gun, but if the other rabbits saw him there would be a quick thud-thud and an empty field. Where *was* that cat? Surely not still crouching close behind him—so quiet all this time? She must have gone . . .

Suddenly a cold thrill went walking up Dion's spine to the nape of his neck. The rabbit had swung round, ears bolt upright. All the other rabbits reared up, listening. Staring intently through his glasses, Dion saw the red-brown of the hunting fox that had disturbed them as it came slinking in at the upper corner of the field. There was a thud-thud and the three farther rabbits were bolting for the tall hedge;

but one—the nearer one—was coming straight for the place where Dion waited. In one movement the gun was up to his shoulder, the barrel swinging to trap the rabbit in its sights. The rabbit was racing down the shadow border, beside the dark high hedge—thirty yards, twenty-five yards, another three for safety, and the air cracked with the sound of sudden gunfire. Everything happened in a shatter of a second. With a high sideways leap Dion's rabbit had vanished into a crimson bramble in the hedge-bottom. The whole field was empty—no rabbits, no fox. All had disappeared as if into the quiet sunlit air.

Dion was on his feet now, making for the bramble; but the cat was already ahead of him. He had forgotten her for a moment, but there she was; tail high and bristling like a little Christmas tree, head up, sniffing excitedly— like a small war-horse, Dion thought, hurrying after her, like the one in the book of Job who "saith among the trumpets, Ha, ha; and he smelleth the battle afar off." One would really think that she *liked* the noise and excitement of gunfire—the old battle-axe!

At the hedge the cat was sniffing round the bramble bush, walking up and down the dewy grass on stiff, tense paws, her eyes like chips of bright blue lightning.

"Is it there, Vashti? Seek it lass!" said Dion, as one might speak to a gun-dog. But Vashti went on stalking stiffly up and down, every muscle tightened with excitement. Propping his gun carefully into the hedge, Dion bent to peer inside the bramble. Nothing to be seen but the shadows of the cobwebbed leaves that still clung, reddening, to the twigs. He tried from a different angle, and then from another, and this time he saw distinctly the white blob that couldn't, surely, be anything else than the scut of his dead rabbit. He had *thought* he'd got it, when it made that curious leap, a leap that had landed it in this prickly shadowy place so difficult for ungloved hand to reach.

"Cat!" He used the odd pet-name by which she was often called at home: it sounded comically abrupt, but suited her personality, especially when glorified a little to "O Cat!"

"Cat! Go and fetch it!"

But she, inscrutable, maddening animal, was now sitting calmly washing the wetness from her paws. She looked at him with a slow blink as if to say, "What about some more excitement like the last lot?" But did she do anything about the rabbit in the bush? On the contrary, for all the interest she displayed there might not have been a rabbit nearer than the Punch Bowl.

"My good animal! If you're coming around with me I'm going to see you earn your company. Why should I get all the skin scratched off my hands when you are here? Now"—he picked her up and thrust her nose-first into the bramble—"jolly well get it!"

There was a great deal of snuffling and sniffing in the hedge-bottom, accompanied by encouraging remarks from Dion, but after some minutes the cat returned again, pressing her way through the prickly twigs with her dark-pointed ears laid flat along her head. She had examined the rabbit and abandoned it. She might almost have been saying, "It's no good, it's only a dead one," thought Dion, exasperated.

"I *know* it's a dead one, you lunatic! I shot it. Go on back and fetch it *out*!"

He put her back into the bush again, beginning to wonder why he was bothering with her at all. After all, a gun-cat! You never heard of them. The idea was perfectly ridiculous; they only sat about and washed the wetness off their elegant paws instead of getting on with the business the way a gun-dog would. But after all, he reflected, listening and peering, you had to train a gun-dog before you began to get the slightest results. And—yes—judging by the dragging noises and the fierce, muffled growling, his gun-cat *was* retrieving, after all her feigned indifference.

Staring through his glasses into the gloom of the bramble, Dion saw the whiteness of her flank. The rabbit was a full-grown one, very heavy for so small a cat. She couldn't lift it from the ground, but she had it firmly by the scruff and was dragging it, inch by inch, her ferociousness and jungle instincts roused by contact with the prey. Filtering through the fur of the rabbit's scruff was a non-stop curiously high-pitched growling.

Gosh, thought Dion, I hope she doesn't eat it before I get my hands on it.

But in this respect Vashti was all a gun-cat should be. She didn't eat game she hadn't killed herself—at least, not unless it was disguised as dinner in a dish. Edging her way slowly clear of the bush she released her hold of Dion's rabbit, sat down and resumed the cleaning of her paws. The only interest she still had for the rabbit was shown in her continuous small growl, while washing, and in a quick dab with one black paw when Dion bent to pick it up. But she made no real claim to it, and was content for him to have it. When he turned out of the field again, the gun under his arm, the rabbit dangling, she was trotting at his heels. Plainly, it was the sport that she wanted, not the rabbit. There was no doubt about it—she was a born battle-axe if ever there was one.

Walking up the slope to the birch coppice to lay his snares, Dion noticed Peter down in the broom thicket, banging in a tethering-peg with his heel. I bet he'll be surprised, he thought, when I tell him we've got a promising gun-cat! So will they all! He was taking the used cartridge out of the breach of his gun and slipping in a new one.

The dew was falling again already, so short were these autumn days; and down in the deep valley the mist came floating up in lazy spirals. On the wind, coming and going, were the two sweet notes of the cow-bells—ding-dong, ding-ding-dong. So the heifers were all right still. And tomorrow was another day from school. All was well with his world.

CHAPTER FIVE

The Cunning of the Beast

THROUGHOUT the long drowsy evening of lamplight and firelight Dion's world still seemed to be a very good one. The family was all together in the large sitting-room, where the floor was so old it rose up into a high bump in the middle—like the back of a basking whale, except for the carpet being goldy-brown—and where the night-black windows were shadowed in the depths of thick stone walls. The chairs and comfortably-sagging sofa were drawn up round the crackle and dance of a wood fire piled on fire-dogs in the cave of the open fireplace, which was built of little rose-red bricks time-out-of-mind ago.

To begin with, Lindsey was more happy in her mind about Freyni's leg, having done everything that could be done for it, so her anxiety no longer hung about the house making everyone else's mind uneasy, in the way anxiety does. She was sprawling in a corner of the sofa, with Freyni on her knee and sheets of recorder music everywhere, and she was practising the Pastoral from the Corelli *Christmas Concerto*.

Peter, too, had at last stopped worrying everyone, for the time being, with schemes for catching Mr. Muncher and was supposed to be doing his homework.

"D'you know what the bass clef looks like?" he was saying conversationally to Lindsey. "It's just like the pupae of the common gnat; I had to draw one at school today."

"Of course I do," said Lindsey, removing her recorder to say it. "Now jolly well get on with your homework, and let me concentrate on this."

Mrs. Thornton was writing a letter to Andrea, her pad balanced uncomfortably on the arm of her chair because Vashti was lying on her knee. The letter was mostly about

Vashti, as it happened, for her exploits as a gun-cat had been the talk of the family since Dion and Peter had come home at tea-time, with the rabbit and the cat and all the news.

". . . I think perhaps she was trying to make up to us for having lost Glen, poor dog," she was writing. "Dion thinks she might become really useful, if he can find time to train her a little, but now Holleybone doesn't come so often as he used to, poor Dion seems always to be busy."

"I just can't get over that cat," remarked Mr. Thornton suddenly, looking up from a block covered with rough sketches of different kinds of fish.

"I know, dear, I was just writing about her to Andrea. Shall I give her your love?"

"Oh, yes, of course. You know, I dare say she's probably the only case of a genuine gun-cat in the whole of the world today."

"Yes, dear, I expect so," said Mrs. Thornton, sorting this out. "You know, George, I was just thinking; it would be rather nice if we could afford to have Holleybone back as often as we used to—or even every other day. He could do the milking for Dion in term-time, and the feeding and mucking-out and all the rest. It's such a lot for the children to do, as well as school and homework."

"Conversationally speaking," said Mr. Thornton, "the way this family leaps from branch to branch is most spectacular. What has Holleybone to do with Vashti? Not that it matters, since we really can't afford to have him so often as we have him now."

"I expect she's got him in her letter," suggested Peter helpfully.

"Well, as it happens, I have. Peter darling, I do think you'd get on better with your homework in the kitchen."

"Oh, I'm all right, Mother, thanks. And—well—I say, Mother, now I'm nine I do feel a bit old to be called darling. I mean, it's awfully nice here at home, of course, but if any of the other chaps were around they might think I was pretty sissy. I mean, it would be awful if you said it at school! But do go on saying it at home—unless you think you ought to practise *not* saying it, of course." Feeling

47

rather bogged at this point, Peter wavered to a stop. It could be painful, growing up.

"All right, dar—I mean Peter, I understand perfectly!" His mother twinkled comfortably over her letter, thus sweeping away any doubts Peter might have had about hurting her feelings. "I ought to have thought of it myself, but when you're my age time goes by at such a rate; it only seems a few months ago that you were falling out of the pram."

Looking back over Andrea's letter to her to see if there were any questions she hadn't answered, she suddenly smiled.

"Andrea says," she said, looking up at Dion, who was throwing logs on the fire till the sparks flew upwards, " 'Tell Dion I haven't driven anything at all since his old tractor, except people mad; but in the summer people sometimes get a chance at the motor mower.' "

"She'll like to hear about Vashti," said Dion, taking off his glasses and polishing them on a corner of his handkerchief.

Lindsey stopped in the middle of a bar. "If you're telling her about Freyni, tell her we think she's getting better. And tell her I can play the Dance of the Sugar Plum Fairy —except for the twiddly bits, because they're for the bass clef. I do wish," she added hopefully to Peter, "that someone else in this house could play, to do the diddle-iddle-*pom* bits."

"Why not try playing two recorders? You've got that old black one."

"I have tried, but it only makes your mouth stretch, so that it feels funny for hours afterwards, and half the time it only goes down one recorder. Besides, you do really need more hands to do it properly, because of having twice as many stops."

Dion said, "In ten minutes it's that play about Nansen and the *Fram*."

"I'll stop in ten minutes, then. Peter how does the *Flower Waltz* go?"

Peter hummed a little self-consciously.

"Don't be silly, that's the *Blue Danube*!"

48

Lindsey shut her eyes, frowned, and tried to play it from memory.

"Well, *that's* the *Blue Danube*, too!" Peter was indignant.

"I know, it keeps coming that way."

"Well, why not *play* the *Blue Danube*, then? Anyway, if I've only got five minutes to finish my homework before Nansen, I'd better get down to it, so jolly well shut up."

"Peter!" said his mother firmly. "Any more of that and you will *have* to do it in the kitchen."

Dion picked up the *Radio Times* and began to study the cast of the play. He was more than ever conscious of an all's-well feeling: perhaps because the sort of family life which has common enough affection to tolerate a smatter of straight talking is always on the whole a good one. But the trouble with a private world in which all goes well, is that all cannot possibly keep on going well. In Dion's case the natural swing-back of the pendulum began in the early hours of the next morning.

He had set the alarm clock for just after five, in order to go up to the high fields with Peter and do the round of his rabbit snares well before dawn, for the foxes left little to be found by late risers. It was no use including Lindsey in this kind of expedition, for she always looked the other way whenever they reached a snare and wouldn't help to carry the dead rabbits if she could avoid it.

Dion was awake before the alarm went off. He so hated the sudden shrill clamour of it that, on mornings when he had to use it, he generally woke himself in time to press down the little knob on the top of the clock and so prevent the onset of the uproar. The curious thing was, he reflected, fumbling sleepily for his slippers, he could never be sure of waking *without* the knowledge that the alarm was set.

Peter was still asleep at the other side of the room: Dion's torch showed up the hump of his blankets and the tousle of his brown hair on the pillow.

"Come on, wake up, Peter! Rabbit snares!"

With a long scri-itch noise Dion struck a match and held it to the candle on the window ledge. The candle flame rose up from a flicker to a full pointed petal of fire, and the boys' bedroom stood out like a stage set in the dramatic darks and lights of candle illumination.

Peter was difficult to awaken, but if Dion had gone without him he would have been wild with disappointment, so as there was no time for niceties and the human voice had no more effect than the alarm, Dion pulled back Peter's blankets with one strong sweep and let the cold October morning do the work for him.

After Peter had got over his first miseries at being wrenched so cruelly into consciousness, he began to feel pleasantly excited at the prospect of being out and about so long before anyone else. At least, not quite before anyone else: the Faithfuls at Rockfield Farm would already be up, of course, like most other dairy farmers, for they had to see that the churns were filled and standing ready by the gate before the milk lorry passed.

Dion was dressed first.

"I'll go and hunt out some bread and cheese; it's hours to breakfast. Don't wake them all up, will you, when you come down. That iron door-latch is a snorter if you clank it."

"All right," said Peter, tugging at his trousers. "I say, I do believe there's a mist."

"Generally is at this time of year."

Peter watched him vanish into the black pit of the staircase, and a minute later plunged down it himself; but he had the candle so that the staircase became a flickery twisty tunnel. The treads groaned and cracked aloud, and Peter was suddenly assailed by his old exciting fear that one day it would utterly collapse and pitch him steeply down into the blackness of the cellar.

In the kitchen Dion had lit the storm lantern and hung it on a nail up in the rafters. It cast a circular black shadow on the red tiles of the floor, and an oily smoky smell upon the air.

He was cutting brown bread at the table. The cats were eating cheese-rind on the coloured drugget mat; at least Vashti was. Freyni was sitting by the Aga, taking no interest, and Peter was rather afraid that Lindsey had been too hopeful about her leg the night before.

50

"Sling on something warm," said Dion, clamping bread-lids on the sandwiches and pushing them into a paper bag. "It's colder than you'd think."

"I hope Mr. Muncher found an empty earth somewhere," said Peter, finding his old gloves underneath a pocketful of oddments.

In the kitchen Dion had lit the storm lantern

"Rucksack," said Dion, reaching for it up among the bridles on the wall. "Lantern, cartridges, gun. Vashti won't want to come in all this damp."

"Mist's lifting," said Peter as they went out.

"Patchy, I expect. Look at it lying in Barn field, just like wool in the moonlight."

"You can hear it dripping in the yew tree."

"What's much more cheering is that you can hear the heifers' bells. Listen! So they're still all right."

The sound of them floating out from the thickness of the mist in Barn field was muffled, like bells of old churches drowned beneath the sea.

"Jolly well is cold," said Peter.

They were going up the steep track into Yew Tree field,

Peter cheerfully swinging the lantern: they were level with the bedroom windows of the farmhouse, then with the steep mossy roof. The dark house was swirled about with moonlit streamers of the mist; then it was past and below them, and they were up on Yew Tree field, where the hens were housed in two movable arks upon the grass.

"Nice and clear up here," said Peter. "It's one of those mists that lie in hollows. Jim Faithful says they mean fine weather."

Dion wasn't listening. He had stopped and was staring at the dark triangles of the poultry-arks under the moon.

"What's the——" began Peter, looking over his shoulder. "Oh, crikey!"

They were running over the wet grass, rabbit-snares forgotten. Dion was saying, "And I never heard a thing! Not a *thing*."

All round the arks the dead hens lay, like molehills in the moonlight. Dion bent over them in silence, lifting one and then another, their feathers drifting loosely to the grass.

Peter swung his lantern over the dreadful scene, wishing and wishing that disaster could leave the farm alone, for everyone's sake, but much more for Dion's because he loved it so: but it was first one thing and then another.

"One fox," said Dion bitterly, "and all this! They don't kill to eat, they do it for the fun of it."

Peter was lifting the lantern and peering into the arks.

"I think they're all all right in this one!"

Dion looked up from the dead bird in his hands.

"They would be; they're all the old ones. Think of the cunning of the beast! Picking out every young one and leaving the old boilers. All our young pullets—every one!"

"I think there's *one* left——" Peter was peering into the other ark, and Dion came and stared across his shoulder.

"Gosh, yes! One survivor. It's that odd-coloured one, too."

"The one that looks like a pheasant. I say, fancy being the sole survivor of all this massacre! She must feel like the Last of the Mohicans."

Dion shrugged. "Never mind what she feels like, she's
52

all right now. Think of what we'll feel like—no eggs to speak of all the winter. Those old birds are past it, they're only fit for eating now."

"Well, there's one pullet." Peter tried to put a better face on things, but Dion said, "What is one among so many?" and began to gather up the corpses. Peter helped him, rather hating the job because it was casting gloom upon the dewy pleasantness of their morning, and because it was postponing the thrill of walking round the snares, like poachers in the mist before dawn.

"There's one thing," said Dion, straightening up with a pair of pullets dangling from each hand, "we'll have to move the arks down into the yard for the winter. No good putting them on good grass at the cost of all their lives."

"You'd never think," said Peter, marvelling, "that any fox could have got into those arks. I mean, they're jolly strongly built, almost new, in fact."

"That's what I thought. The only thing now is to keep the poultry nearer to the house. Foxes won't usually come very near houses, and if they do, someone would hear and get out quickly enough to stop most of the damage."

"It seems a pity," said Peter as they trudged back down the track, burdened with the leavings of the massacre, "that there isn't a hunt anywhere round here."

"There're more ways than one of killing foxes. Did you hear that the Faithfuls lost four geese last week, and fifteen cockerels in September? And the poultry farm down the lane lost nearly forty layers last winter. Holleybone says the farmers are talking about organising a series of fox-shoots this year, and if they do I hope they come round this way; I'll be with them."

"Where are we putting all these hens?" asked Peter hopefully. "Because if we don't get round the snares pretty quickly now, we'll find the foxes have had all our rabbits as well."

"All right, dump them here on the bank. We'll take them in when we get back."

On the grassy bank opposite the quiet farmhouse the dead hens were stacked. They looked like a heap of brown-gold feathers in the lantern-light, Peter thought; but Dion was

53

thinking how he had set the eggs under two broody hens, away back in the last Easter holidays; how he had watched them hatch into small fluffy yellow balls, and then grow into long-legged, scraggy-feathered flappers; how he had fed and cared for them, moving them daily on to fresh green grass, watering them and cleaning out their houses, until finally they had grown to be beautiful sleek-feathered Rhode-Sussex pullets, on the point of beginning their long first season of laying. Some, indeed, had been laying already. Dion had been proud of these pullets; they had been as good as any in the neighbourhood, and he had reared them almost alone, in what spare time he could snatch from school and other farm work.

And now this . . .

A heap of brown-gold feathers on the bank beside the track.

"Come on," said Dion. "Or there'll be no time before the milking."

CHAPTER SIX

Solitary Survivor

THE fact that there was only one good rabbit in the snares did nothing to enliven the feeling of depression at breakfast in the kitchen that morning, for there had also been the remains of four other rabibts, raided in the wires by foxes, who had left only a scut here and a head there to show the true haul of Dion's and Peter's snaring.

Mr. Thornton had not missed the opportunity of remarking again that Dion was undertaking more than he could manage, and also of working out the cost to the farm of the loss of fourteen point-of-lay pullets.

Dion himself said very little, because there seemed nothing to say that could possibly make anyone feel any better. Lindsey was full of a renewed anxiety about Freyni's swollen leg, which added to the general despondency, and whatever conversation Peter started, it was squashed in early infancy. Mrs. Thornton did her best to raise the family's spirits without falling into the dreadful error of artificial brightness, but even her remark that several of the less damaged hens seemed reasonably fit for cooking only added to Dion's sense of loss—that one should think of his fine pullets in terms of chicken dinners—so everyone was relieved when the meal was ended and gloom could be sunk in bursts of activity. Mrs. Thornton, aware of the swift melting away of all her family, looked up from the perusal of rabbit and chicken recipes and called them back.

"Lindsey! Dishes first, darling. And Peter, it's your turn to do the sitting-room carpet, you know. Dion, you haven't made your bed yet, have you? And I'd like you to bring me some coke from the outside cellar, please."

"Oh, Mother! I must do Freyni's leg first. Are you sure we really oughtn't to get the vet? She hasn't eaten any breakfast."

"I'll have a look at her in a minute, dear. Peter, don't forget to do the rug and under the sofa."

"Oh, Mother! With all these foxes about, I do think I ought to have a go at Mr. Muncher again, first!"

"It won't take you ten minutes to do the carpet—and you never know who might come and find it in a state. Oh, and Dion, you haven't got your glasses on. You know you simply must keep on with them if you want to get your eyes right again. Yes, I know it was misty this morning, and that it clouds the lenses, but it isn't misty here in the kitchen—or even outside now."

What with one thing and another the morning was well advanced before the tyranny of the house could be left behind and the real business of the day begun. For Peter this meant a renewed attack on the perilous freedom of Mr. Muncher, beginning with a careful stalking sortie in order to establish his present whereabouts, and ending (he hoped) with a triumphant capture in a concealed pit which he would dig at a likely spot in the probable path of his rabbit.

"And fill it in afterwards, of course," he added hastily, seeing Dion's face.

"I should jolly well hope so, too. Can't you help me down with the ark and the old hens first?"

"Really Dion, with Mr. Muncher in hourly danger from all those foxes I shouldn't have thought you'd ask. And after all, what about you helping me with him? Not that you would, of course."

"I should think not! Putting a rabbit before thirteen useful hens. Anyway, Lindsey'll give me a hand."

"But I was going to ask her to help me drive Mr. Muncher across my pit-trap! And first you say the hens are too old for anything but eating, and then you say they're useful!"

Dion looked at him for a moment, on the point of a crushing answer but thinking better of it.

"If you'll give me a hand down with the ark and the hens, I'll help you afterwards with your rabbit."

"Oh—all right, then. Lindsey's in the stable with the colt; shall I call her?"

"Yes, see if she can come; we'll finish much quicker with three of us."

Lindsey came, but she was plainly on edge to get back again to the stable.

"You see, someone's simply got to take Chalice out this morning. He has to have his leading lesson (he's still terribly bad at that) and, much more important, he should have grass and exercise; he's been kept in ever since they all broke out oñ Friday evening. You know, Dion, we'll just have to turn him out again tomorrow. We'll all be at school and no one to take him out, and at his age he needs the exercise and grazing, and the sunshine, too, I expect."

They were walking up to Yew Tree field, and Dion was carrying the cats' travelling basket for the transporting of the hens.

"If we have to turn him out," he said, "I suppose we just have to. But another night's tramping round the Punch Bowl after lost animals won't work in very well with Monday's homework."

"Perhaps he won't break out again," said Lindsey. "I shouldn't think he would: I mean, surely he must be getting a bit more used to being without his mother, every day."

"And even if he does, you'll find them all much quicker now the heifers have their bells on," said Peter.

"It's all very well for you to talk; you know you won't be allowed out to help find them, in an evening," said Dion.

They came to the top of the steep track and turned sharply out into the high green field that took its name from the majestic triple yew tree growing on its brink, reaching above the highest chimney of the farmhouse.

"Look at the gossamer!" said Lindsey in sudden delight. "Everywhere! All over the grasses, and shining with the dew."

"Look at the empty poultry-ark," said Dion, "and all the feathers in your lovely gossamer."

"You're being morbid," Lindsey said. "Those things don't mean we can't enjoy beautiful things."

"And the ark isn't empty—not quite," Peter pointed out. "There's the last of the Mohicans, the sole survivor of the plot."

57

They stood and looked at this solitary bird. Sitting huddled in a sunny corner with a dazed expression in her small eyes, her gold-brown feathers ruffled, she looked as much like a drunken duchess after a tussle as anything else.

Lindsey said suddenly, "I'm glad it was the pheasant-looking bird, she has such lovely plummage. I always liked her, ever since I saw she was so different from the others. And she's already started laying, too."

"Well, make a start with her," said Dion. "Here's the basket. Then Peter and I can get that ark on the way. They're supposed to be mobile, but they're jolly heavy, unless you're tough and strong as Holleybone. We'll have to keep resting rather a lot, I expect, before we get it to the yard."

"Pity he isn't here now," said Peter. "When he only comes on Tuesdays and Thursdays we never see him, except in the holidays, and I wanted to ask him about Mr. Muncher. He'd be sure to have a notion."

Lindsey opened the small door of the ark and crept inside among the drifted feathers with the basket. The odd-coloured pullet made little effort to dodge her grasping fingers, and soon she was safely stowed inside the basket with the lid shut down.

"I've got her!"

"Good, now see how many of the old ones you can squash in as well. They won't mind, for a few minutes, and it'll save you extra journeys," Dion said. "Ready, Peter? Grap the rope that's fixed at your end and heave."

It was nearly an hour's job, establishing the whole surviving hen population safely in the farmyard. The old hens were not nearly so easy to catch as the pheasant-bird had been, and Lindsey got very hot and flustered, diving about in the low-roofed ark in the midst of cackling, squawking, flapping hens who went straight into hysterics every time her hand went near them.

"It was shock that kept the pullet so quiet," said Dion when they stopped at last and stood to look at the completed exodus.

"She's still suffering from it now," said Peter. "Look at

her, all huddled in the corner, just the way she was in Yew Tree field. One of my hamsters did that for the whole of one morning, the day she escaped and Vashti caught her."

"Poor thing!" said Lindsey pitifully. "Can't we do something for her? What do they tell you to give for shock in first-aid books?"

"For people, you mean?" asked Dion. "Oh, hot tea and keep them warm, I think. I never heard of anything for hens!"

"Well, if she isn't any better after I've come back with Chalice I'll get some for her. She'd be easy to wrap up in a little blanket, and I could spoon some tea down her, the way you do with medicine."

"Did Mother tell you about Chalice's nipping?" Dion called after her as she turned to race towards the stable.

"No, what? I mean, naturally I know he does nip."

"Well, it was the laundryman last. And Mother said he said he wouldn't come up here any more if it happened again."

"Oh, help! I thought Chalice was getting better."

She frowned perplexedly, kicking the toe of her wellington in the dry mud.

"Well, Mother says you've got to hit him *hard* every time he does it now, and if that doesn't stop him he'll have to wear a muzzle."

"Oh, but then he couldn't graze!"

"It's what she said." Dion looked at her, wishing she could be a little harder-hearted—just a little, because it was simply no use at all being over tender-hearted on a farm. "You'd better just bring yourself to clout him, good and hard," he said, and it was the best advice he had.

"Now Mr. Muncher," Lindsey heard Peter saying as she went into the stable.

The colt spun round from his hay-net in the corner and whickered at her hopefully. He looked so adorable, the small wanderer, like a large woolly toy—it was impossible to think of him as having any vice. She was sure he hadn't, it was all meant only in play. She looked at the soft pink-striped, comically-whiskered muzzle and hated the thought of hitting it—hitting it hard. It would be like slapping the

59

face of a baby. But there was no getting away from it, plainly it would have to be done, in order to save him from the worse miseries of wearing a muzzle.

She reached up for his little leather foal-slip, and hesitated for a moment, swinging it in her two hands. Ought she, perhaps, to dash up to the house and have another look at Freyni first? Ought she really to have rendered first aid to the pheasant-bird *before* taking Chalice out; or would afterwards be soon enough? Or was she possibly just putting off Chalice's lesson in case she had to bring herself to hit him? It was so difficult knowing the truth about anything; even (or perhaps especially) about oneself.

A second whicker, and a little delighted buck-jump across his box, decided Lindsey to get on with Chalice's lesson. It would be too awful to disappoint him now, when he was so excited and pleased at the thought of going out again after all his hours in the stable.

She ducked under the dividing pole and began to buckle on the foal-slip. It was such a lovely, light, pliable thing; much nicer than a head-collar. The colt was good at having things done to him, and he stood quietly while she fitted it on his head.

"It's your own fault, Chalice darling," she was saying to him, in the way that all the Thorntons talked to all of their animals. "If only you wouldn't *do* these awful things you'd find life so much easier. No breaking-out, no keeping you in; no nipping, no hitting—see?"

Chalice blew down her neck.

If only he doesn't nip while I've got my back turned, thought Lindsey, bending to slide and lower the pole that shut him in. He didn't nip and Lindsey, with a sigh of relief, led him out into the sunshine. Four steps, and suddenly he stopped; little hoofs stuck firmly into the mud of the track, his head held high and stubborn. Who would have thought, said Lindsey to herself, that he'd been longing to get out? But he had. She knew that. It was just his natural cussedness.

"Come on, Chalice, don't be silly!"

She tugged persistently, with short strong pulls, at his head. Then suddenly he walked on, just as if he had never thought of stopping. This was a fine free walk with a long stride, smooth and fast. Lindsey walked beside him light-heartedly, hoping her mother might possibly be at one of the easterly windows as they passed the old farmhouse on their way down the track past the Swing Tree. Her father wouldn't, of course; he was still wholly absorbed in his fishes, and the Thornton children had realised for years how hopeless it was to expect him to take any proper interest in other things when he was working on a book.

Chalice stuck in all four hoofs and stopped

The sun was warm, and the colouring of the high hedge by the Swing Tree was glorious as fire. The hedge swung outwards, arching over the double wheel-tracks like a breaking wave, a wave of melted copper; and under the glory of it Chalice walked so well and willingly that Lindsey looked suddenly backwards, still hoping for a face at a window, to see the almost-miracle of the colt's sweet reasonableness before it left him with a rush.

It was difficult to see a face at the inside of a window, when you are outside and the sun is shining. But the house itself looked suddenly so beautiful, with its old grey walls all hung with waving honeysuckle stems, and its sweeping roof encrusted with green mosses and looking like the swell on a summer sea; Lindsey felt it was the one and perfect symbol of all homes. Whenever anyone said the word "home" to her, through all the rest of her life, she thought, it was this that she would see in her mind's eye; the old house in the sunlight, the flaming arch above the way to it, and the full black skirts of the triple yew tree, high above, and behind it.

Everything's so perfect it almost hurts, thought Lindsey, walking beside Chalice; I won't remember Freyni, and the little hen, and the colt's breaking-out—not just for another minute, while it's still a magic moment.

"Hey!" yelled a voice from the heights of Hanger field. "Has he nipped you yet? Dion says if he has he hopes you clouted him properly."

"He hasn't, he's being perfect," Lindsey called back softly, enchantment crashing round her ears. Well, it was probably all for the best; she was always being accused of being too dreamy.

Peter's head was just visible in a gap in Hanger field hedge, his hair looking like an old yard brush.

"We can't get near old Muncher. Isn't it a rotten shame? But we're digging a wonderful pit-trap."

Lindsey made a vague movement intended to mean, "I can't keep shouting back because of Chalice; isn't he walking wonderfully?"

Peter, thinking it meant "Shut up," disappeared behind the hedge again, and suddenly Chalice stuck in all four hoofs and stopped with such a jerk that Lindsey almost lost her balance. Anyone who understood horses could have seen at once what it was the colt was saying:

"Grass! Don't you *know* I've been shut in for hours and hours? Grass!"

"All right," said Lindsey. "But not now—this minute. Six steps first, and then I'll let you stop and graze."

She saw he did it, too, though it took her five minutes and a whole world of patience, when so much else was clamouring to be seen to. But it would never do, she well knew, to let him stop when he suggested it, for in the training of young animals it was only at the will of the trainer that a thing might be done or not be done.

Meanwhile Dion and Peter, having dug the trap-hole and covered it cunningly with twigs and fallen leaves and grass, were getting very hot and blown in trying to head off Mr. Muncher from all the wildly unsuitable directions he wished to take, so that they could drive him through the gap where the little pit was secretly awaiting him. Mr. Muncher was very unco-operative. No amount of shouting, running, tip-toeing, enticing, stick-throwing, or arm-waving seemed to have any effect at all in convincing him that their idea might at least be as good as some of his. After about an hour of this kind of thing, Peter thought that he would never again run very fast anywhere without mentally seeing, out of the corner of his eye, an exasperating piebald rabbit dodging diagonally across his path. Dion decided at about the same time that he had had quite enough of the thing, and had given Peter at least as much time over the rabbit as Peter had given him over the poultry.

"Oh, you might just stay a little longer! One person is absolutely useless driving a rabbit by himself."

"So are two people," said Dion, blowing on his glasses and polishing them with his handkerchief. "So probably would ten be, or even a hundred. He just doesn't want to be driven, and he knows perfectly well what we're after. Besides, I've got to go round Barn field hedges, if we're turning that colt out again tonight."

"Oh, Dion! Can't you put him in Lower Naps with the ponies and Duchess?"

"No, not after Nanti kicked him. And he'd break out just as easily from there as from anywhere else; and where would we be with the ponies and the milk-cow gadding half across the country?"

Peter stood forlornly staring at the distant scut of Mr. Muncher bobbing cheerfully down towards the bottom of the steep hill of Hanger field, where the grass grew greener and deeper.

"What with the foxes, and the Faithfuls' dog, and everything—even the cats hunt rabbits."

"I shouldn't worry, old chap. Bet you they won't touch

him, he's so odd-looking. Give him a few days of rain or frost or something equally uncomfortable, and you'll have him eating out of your hand. I suppose you wouldn't help me with the hedges? There may be several places needing strengthening."

"Well, I might have, but I think I'd better see if Lin will help me with old Muncher."

Dion could have said a great deal at that moment about lack of co-operation on the farm, but after all Peter was only nine, and not even really interested in farming except as a delightful background to his own occupations, or as a source of cream and eggs and butter, or a place to keep a pony. When he was older—if he wasn't bullied about too much now—he might be a real help, and with twice the strength he had now. And there was always Lindsey.

Lindsey, however, was of little use to either of them that morning. When they reached the farmyard she had got back with Chalice but was now squatting on a handle of the wheelbarrow holding the pheasant-bird, well wrapped up in a bit of old blanket, on her knee. Inside the wheelbarrow was a cup without a handle, and out of it Lindsey was spooning something brown which she slowly dribbled inside the pullet's beak.

"Oh, there you are!" she said in a relieved voice. "I'm so glad, because it's terribly awkward holding her beak open with one hand and spooning tea down with the other, and keeping her in the blanket, all at the same time. We could really do with all three of us. Oh, and Dion, we can't put her back in the ark with all the old birds, they were bullying her to death—pecking her and driving her in corners—and it must have made her shock much worse, poor thing."

"Yes, I rather expected that," said Dion. "They never mix well, different ages; but on the other hand they don't do well alone."

"Even solitary confinement's better than persecution," said Lindsey, settling the bird more closely in the blanket.

"Oh, well, perhaps you're right; we can try it. Pity about all this, though. I was hoping you would come hedging."

"*Well*, of all the——" began Peter, but Lindsey said that

64

if he shouted like that he'd undo all her work with the pullet.

"Anyone *would* shout," he said defensively. "*I* said I was going to ask you first! To help me catch old Muncher."

Lindsey stirred the sweet tea, and spooned a few more dribbles down the pullet's yellow beak. "Then you might just as well both stop arguing; because when I've done this I've got to fix up the other ark for this hen, so that she can live in peace; and after that I've got to do Freyni again, and by that time it will be dinner. But there's always the afternoon. Oh, and by the way, I must tell you!" She suddenly grinned. "Jim Faithful's just been round to say did we know Peter's rabbit is out?"

c

CHAPTER SEVEN

Vast Jig-Saw Puzzle

ALL that afternoon Lindsey had helped Dion with the hedges in Barn field, and Peter, failing to get anyone to help him with his rabbit, had suddenly tired of the whole thing and gone riding on Sula in the Punch Bowl.

After tea the whole family tidied themselves up and walked down the winding lane to church, a mile away in the village.

"I had to get ready in rather a rush," Mrs. Thornton was saying. "I do hope my hat is on all right? The worst of not usually wearing one is that you lose track of the fashionable tilts and angles."

"The *hat's* all right, Mother darling," Lindsey said, screwing her eyes up at it in the moonlight. "It's your hair that really looks old-fashioned. I think it's those long side bits; you ought to have them trimmed, or brushed back, or something."

Dion said, "Yes, you're right about the hair. Lin, but *not* about the hat; it needs to be at least five degrees to south'ard. Stand still a moment, Mother—now—like this!"

"Well, really——" said Mrs. Thornton.

"The total lack of respect you children have for both your parents," said Mr. Thornton, turning round in the middle of the lane, "is simply disgraceful!"

Peter grinned suddenly. "You can't *have* respect for really human people."

"Now, if you were a pompous Victorian sort of father," said Dion, walking backwards to study the angle of the hat, "we might be so awestruck and terrified we'd *seem* as respectful as anyone could be."

"And go on walking to church, Sunday after Sunday, with Mother's hat looking just like a cowl on a chimney," said Peter, "and never dare to say a word about it."

66

"I might try it some day," said Mr. Thornton thoughtfully. "It would be worth the strain, just to see you people subdued."

This Sunday evening was starting out very much like any other Sunday evening, but before they had left the village for home again both Dion and Lindsey had become involved in things that no one had expected. With Lindsey, the wheels of her mind had begun to move before the service had properly begun, while she sat waiting with the quiet congregation listening to the music of the organ. Like waves it was, she thought, like waves that swept up full and majestic, and crashed in thunder at your feet. She wondered why she had never really listened to it before—not listened as she was listening now.

Throughout the service, when the organ played sedately through the prescribed and formal settings for evensong, Lindsey thought a great deal about the way it could be when the music was unharnessed. Now it was like fine horses, stepping in proud obedience in the shafts of coaches; but then, before the service had begun, it was like horses wild and free.

It would be wonderful to let loose with your own fingers the race and leap of music like wild horses. The recorder couldn't do it, she decided sadly, half-way through the first lesson.

"I say, d'you know you've dropped your collection?" Peter hissed suddenly in her ear as she stood up automatically with everyone else for the Magnificat.

"Sh!" said Lindsey, bending to pick it up—how had it got there? But her mind slipped back again at once to what it was absorbed in.

To Dion the organ was an organ. Most probably he didn't give it a thought, for his mind was dealing with the problem of foxes. You could never really be *sure* that they would leave your birds alone, even when the arks were close within the farmyard. Something simply must be done about the foxes. It was a pity they did have this expensive taste for poultry, because if only they would stick to rabbits they would be not only welcome but protected, encouraged, even bred. But poultry—that was quite another thing. Poultry would do very well on the light sandy soil of Punchbowl Farm; one day he hoped to increase them quite a lot. A couple of dozen arks, say, moved daily over the pastures. There would be money in that, and the pastures would benefit enormously besides.

There was no way round it that he could see; the foxes must be kept down. It was a pity there was no hunt, but there wasn't, so other methods must be used, and the best of these, so far as he could see, was shooting. In the church at that moment were at least two neighbouring farmers: he could see Mr. Morton plainly, just in front, and Mr. and Mrs. Bailey out of the corner of his eye if he turned round a shade. There might be others at the back. After the service was over he could stop and talk to Mr. Morton, mentioning the slaughter of the pullets. With any luck they would be in the thick of fixing up a fox-shoot before the Baileys were properly out of ear-shot.

This was exactly what happened, and all before his parents had finished their conversation with the vicar in the porch; before Lindsey had appeared in the doorway after staying to hear the organ to the very end, or Peter from a moonlight inspection of the Murdered Sailor's historic tombstone round the other side of the church. At least, it was almost exactly what happened, but no one needed to shout after Mr. and Mrs. Bailey as they vanished round the corner at the bottom of the hill.

"I'll be seeing him and the others later in the evening," Mr. Morton said. "Funny thing, we'd been thinking of suggesting a shoot up round your way, last time we were out in Beechwood Copse. Three foxes we got that time. But we reckon there are several earths down in your wild valley, in the banks above the stream. Badgers, too; there's lot's of badgers. Did you know?"

"About the badgers? Yes, we've watched them in the evenings, sometimes. But I'm not too sure where the foxes are."

"No, well you mightn't be; they often use badgers' setts, you know. Of course, you can come to know a fox's scent; very strong that is, to those who know it. Well, this won't do. I've a sick cow to look at before I go round for my

68

drink. Saturday afternoon we'll be along, then, if we don't hear any different from you. Good night, Dion."

"Good night, sir! We'll hope for fine weather."

"You ought to come and look at this tombstone!" said Peter's voice, as Peter's shape suddenly emerged from the dark shadow of the church into the moonlight. "It's got the murder all beautifully carved on the front of it, with the sailor felled between the robbers, and a whole lot about 'Here lies a poor unknown sailor——' "

"I know, I've often seen it. What can they be talking about in the porch?"

"Can't imagine, but they're coming now. Look, it's so light you can easily see the conkers on this tree," said Peter, filling his pockets.

There wasn't much opportunity to mention the foxshoot until they were nearly at the farm gate again, because of Lindsey's sudden involvements with the organ.

"Well, you see, Mother, the way it happened was, when Mr. Wingfield stopped playing and saw I was the only one left in the church, he came down the nave and asked me if I wanted anything; so I said no, I'd only stayed to hear the organ; and he said practically no one ever did that—don't you think that's very queer, Mother, when you think how beautifully he plays? You'd think everyone would stay right to the very end."

"You never have, before," said Peter, walking with his head up to see the pattern of leaves against the stars and sky.

"I never really *listened* before, so I didn't realise how well he played."

"Most people never really listen," said her father.

"And perhaps they want to get home and see to their dinners and suppers," said Mrs. Thornton sensibly. "But who suggested lessons first? You know we'll never be able to afford them; you may as well face that fact right at the beginning."

"I don't think anybody quite *suggested* them. I said I wished I could play like that, because though a recorder was nice in its own way, it wasn't at all the same; and he said an organ was a very good thing to learn because there wasn't

69

anything like enough organists for all the schools and churches needing them."

"But that's an indoor job," said Dion, mentally noting that Lower Rockfield Farm was ploughing up old pasture, the furrows showing ribbed with shadow in the moonlight.

"That doesn't matter, for a spare-time job," said Lindsey. "So is milking, if it comes to that. Anyway, what is really important is that after I'd said I didn't think we'd be able to afford for me ever to learn——"

"*Lindsey!*" said Mrs. Thornton, shocked at this casual talk of their poverty.

"Oh, he didn't mind, Mother, really; because he said it was much the same with him; he said practically no one had money in these days. But what *is* important, he said he was very fond of shooting himself (not shooting *himself*, Peter! Stop giggling, you silly ass!), but he thought it was too extravagant—paying for shooting rights, you know."

"So *you* said," remarked Dion, "what about swapping shooting up at your place for organ lessons at yours?"

"I do think," said her father, "that you might consult your mother or me first, before you fix up things like this; if that's what you have done."

"But, Father, I didn't fix anything up! I only said, Oh what a frightfully good thing—that he wanted some shooting, you know—and that perhaps we might be able to arrange something."

"Well, that's as good as fixing up," said Peter.

"It isn't; I only said 'perhaps' and 'might'; and I do think you're all being jolly awkward. I thought everyone would be delighted. Not only because of me learning the organ (which is a thing I can earn money at, later on) but because of all the rabbits. You're always complaining about the rabbits, Dion, the way they spoil your crops and grazings. And last year they barked all your young fruit trees."

"Dad's fruit trees," said Dion conscientiously, though he did do all the work. "He bought them."

"Split-hairer," said Peter. "As if it mattered. Mother bought your trousers, but you never call them hers."

"Well, I dare say the shooting-for-organ-lessons arrangement may be quite all right in a way," said Mrs. Thornton,

70

disregarding the fruit trees and the trousers, "but what I really do think is that you're dabbling in too many instruments. There is your recorder, and you're having violin lessons at school; if you start the organ as well, that'll be less time for the violin——"

"Which she hardly ever practises, as it is," said Mr. Thornton.

"Oh, but Father! I do, at school; it's because it's so awkward carrying it safely backwards and forwards, on pony-back or bicycling, or even walking, that I don't at home very often."

"And you said you were saving up for a flute," said her mother. "I do think it would be much better if you learned one instrument properly."

"Then I think it ought to be the organ," said Lindsey decidedly, "because it's the only one of all the instruments, Mr. Wingfield said, that you can be sure of earning money with. People don't want violinists and flute or recorder players now, unless they're good enough for orchestras, but churches always want organists."

"You'll only drop it for the clavichord, or something, after a year or so," said Dion sagely. "Just the way you've done with all your other instruments."

"I jolly well haven't!" said Lindsey staunchly. "I play them both—and there's only two, after all. You should be thankful we don't go round telling you that you'll only drop farming for medicine, or something."

"Considering I've stuck to farming ever since we came here," remarked Dion, "in spite of school and money-shortage and everything, I shouldn't think anybody *would* say that."

"It's usually a mistake to decide anything in a hurry," said Mr. Thornton. "I suggest we ask Mr. Wingfield to tea, and discuss it then."

"Oh, *Father!* But I wanted to know *now*."

In Lindsey's voice was all the despairing revolt of youth against the slow deliberation of the middle-aged.

"There are a great many things," said her father, "that I also would dearly like to know now; but I have to wait. And, as to the organ lessons, I think you will just have to wait, too, because we can't arrange anything at all without consulting Mr. Wingfield."

"I'm sure it will be all right, dear," said her mother comfortingly to Lindsey, not liking to see her so unsettled with suspense. "Though I do still think to learn one instrument is best."

"Dion will hate to have someone else walking round the fields with a gun," said Peter, jumping shadow-bars of moonlit tree trunks, where they lay across the road.

"As it happens," said Dion, "there'll be quite a lot of people walking round with guns next Saturday, if Dad and Mother don't mind. I was talking to Mr. Morton after church, about the foxes and how we lost our pullets, and he suggested having a fox shoot here on Saturday. They've been doing it on several farms around since September, and he says he thinks there are earths in our wild valley. He said badgers too, but I said we knew about them."

"I think it would be a very good thing, Dion," said his father. "Another raid like the last one and we won't have any poultry left at all."

"*Badgers!*" said Lindsey, utterly forgetting the organ in the urgency of a sudden new fear. "He didn't mean they thought of *shooting* the badgers, did he?"

Dion said, "Probably; I don't know. Lots of people believe they raid poultry houses, so perhaps he did."

"But we know they don't! They don't, do they, Peter? That book we had about them from the library said it was proved they didn't—you read it yourself, Dion! So did Mother and Father. There isn't any case at all against them, and it'd be sheer murder. He's got to tell the men they mustn't shoot the badgers, hasn't he Father?"

"All right, all right, don't go up in flames," said Dion calmly. "As a matter of fact the book did say you sometimes got a sort of rogue badger, that develops a taste for poultry, just as sometimes a tiger turns man-eater. But I shouldn't have thought it mattered very much either way, as there are plenty of badgers there."

Lindsey was shocked to the soul.

"What a dreadful thing to say! As if, when half the people on a liner were drowned, someone said, 'It doesn't matter

72

very much, as there are plenty of others left.' It's all this killing! I suppose it can't be helped with rabbits and foxes and things, that do damage—but when it's an innocent animal, and such a rare one, and so beautiful! You thought how lovely they were yourself, Dion, when we used to go out at dusk and watch them playing in the valley; you can't possibly let them be hurt—can he, Mother—Dad?"

"No, of course not," said Mrs. Thornton, agreeing absolutely. "I think one of the nicest things about our farm is its wildness—so wild that deer and badgers live in the fringes of it."

"Mother, *dear!*" said Dion affectionately. "You wouldn't if you were trying to farm it."

"Nearly home!" Peter sang out, racing right round the little signpost where the lane branched off to the Punch Bowl. "Hot soup and fried snippets in a minute!"

"But Dad!" said Lindsey urgently. "Tell him they musn't touch the badgers! I'll never speak to him again if they shoot any of the badgers."

"Well, on the whole I agree with you and your mother, Lindsey; but I think if there is a case against the badgers we ought to hear it first. I'll ask Mr. Morton when they come up on Saturday."

"Oh, *Father!*"

There were no words to express the maddeningness of grown-up deliberation. How she was going to sleep a wink, or concentrate in school, or give her mind to anything at all, Lindsey simply couldn't imagine, with all the suspense and worry that now hung heavy on it. First there was Freyni's leg, then the colt and his nipping and breaking-out, then the poor shocked pullet, who had still been ruffled and bedazed at church time, despite the blanket and sweet tea treatment; and now there was the matter of the organ and the badgers. It was altogether too much. And people spoke of the carefree days of childhood! Even without the overwhelming difficulties of school, for Lindsey life was a vast jig-saw puzzle from which most of the pieces she was looking for seemed always to be missing.

Swinging in through the farm gateway after Dion and

73

Peter, she suddenly saw the moon-washed pointed roof of the farmhouse, and the great dark globe of the yew tree under the stars, and felt the prickles of her anxiety smoothing down, like a cat's ruffled coat beneath a quiet hand.

CHAPTER EIGHT

Nothing is Ever So Bad ...

MR. WINGFIELD had accepted an invitation to have tea at
Punchbowl Farm on the Wednesday after his conversation
with Lindsey in the church. ("Mother darling, you will brush
back your hair or something, won't you, just before he
comes?" Lindsey asked her mother anxiously at breakfast.)

It had been her turn to ride to school that day, with Dion
on Nanti and Peter making the troublesome journey by
bicycle, riding it where the road and track were good
enough and pushing it where they weren't. The best way for
a bicycle was not the same as the best way for ponies, so
Dion and Lindsey had the Punch Bowl to themselves as
they rode home that day in the level rays of the sinking
sun.

Lindsey's mind was in a state of up-and-downery, quite
common to her, but to her only, of all the Thornton family.
When she thought of Freyni's leg, which would not go down
despite all treatment, and of Freyni's appetite, which
(incredible for her) was so small that you could see her
getting thinner—when she thought of these things Lindsey
was plunged into a pit of apprehensive gloom, not hearing
what Dion was talking about, not even noticing where small
grey Sula was going, nor helping her to choose the smoothest
way between the stones that littered the track. But when she
thought of Chalice, and how he had not led the heifers out
again for nearly a week now, and of the little pheasant-
coloured pullet which had so nicely recovered from her
fright (though she hadn't laid a single egg since the
massacre, and everyone else except Lindsey said she had
gone quite hopelessly mental); when Lindsey thought of
these things, and crowned them with the nice-but-uneasy

knowledge that Mr. Wingfield was coming to tea and so her fate with regard to the organ would finally be settled, then she was as happy as anyone can be.

"Mind that stone!" said Dion suddenly. "I don't believe you're looking where Sula's going at all."

"Oh, sorry, I was thinking. But Sula's footsure as a deer; she never stumbles."

"She might easily with your great weight."

"I do wish you wouldn't talk as if I were a side-show or something."

Dion was gently checking the chestnut Nanti from trying to break into a dancing trot, as she always did do, whether going or coming home. He said patiently, "I didn't mean great in *that* sense; I meant great for Sula. I thought you'd grown out of being so sensitive about that—after all the fuss we had last summer about not eating enough and everything."

"Anyone would think I was *fat*. And I never gallop Sula any more—or jump her either, except over very low things."

"Don't be silly!" said Dion kindly. "Of course you're not fat! But pretty tall, and solid with it. You ought to pick the way for her, you know. Supposing she were dreaming too! You'd both come an awful purler, and she might break her knees."

Lindsey said nothing, realising she was in the wrong. She was carefully watching ahead for Sula's feet now, and swinging her up into the heather to avoid a runnel in the track.

Dion said, "What were you thinking about?"

Looking inwardly at the jumble of her mind, Lindsey selected one suitable item.

"Well, the pullet. Have you noticed how tame she's getting now? I walked right down the yard this morning with her sitting on my wrist—just like a falcon."

"Mental," said Dion, his satchel bumping his back in time to Nanti's springy dancing. "*Walk*, Nanti!"

"Oh, no, I'm sure she isn't! She came when I called her this morning, too. I'd put her down on the dung heap to scratch for worms while I hayed-up the ponies. I often take

76

her about a bit because she's so lonely in that ark all by herself, and Mother won't let her stay loose in case she gets into the garden. She says it's bad enough having Mr. Muncher loose, as he's so tame he's sure to get in when the frosts are bad, if Peter hasn't caught him by then."

Lindsey pressed her legs into Sula's stout sides to catch up with Nanti's lengthening stride.

"I didn't know the pullet had a name to call," said Dion.

"She didn't, when she was only one of so many. But now she's an individual it's so much easier to call her something."

"Such as?"

"Well, I used to call her the pheasant-bird, of course, even before the massacre, because she looked so much like one—I do think her feathers are wonderful, don't you?— but then I thought of looking up 'pheasant' in the dictionary, and it said from the latin Phasiana; so I thought I'd call her Phasian."

There was no point in continuing this conversation any further, as the track narrowed to a horse's width and they would have had to shout, which no one in their right minds would have thought suitable in so wild and splendid a setting as the Devil's Punch Bowl in the latter glories of October. The steep circling sides were avalanches of tumbling, shouting colour. Mists rose tremulously around them, soaked in diffused sunlight like a sorcerer's charm, as if lit by fire from below.

"Fine day tomorrow," said Dion over his shoulder, when the track widened enough for Lindsey to catch up.

"It's so beautiful, you see what it is that makes people want to paint—or write music—or even books."

"In books," said Dion, "I always skip the descriptive bits; all that about how the sunset looked, you know, and woods in springtime. Most people do."

"I don't," said Lindsey. "Not if they're well done, so that you can *see* what was meant. I sometimes read them twice."

"The main thing is to be clear; making people see a

77

thing as you saw it; but you can't just do it by pages of description."

"I know: how on earth I could make Andrea say, see how the Punch Bowl looks just now, I can't imagine."

"It's a bit different from last Friday night!" said Dion with a dry grin. "Didn't it rain!"

"And blow," said Lindsey. "You know, when I think that Chalice and the heifers haven't broken out once since that night, I hardly dare believe it."

Mr. Wingfield was just going in at the garden gate when Dion and Lindsey rode into the yard. He said, "Good afternoon! Do you know there's a black-and-white rabbit loose in the orchard?"

"Oh, yes," said Lindsey, slithering from her saddle. "It's Peter's; it escaped. I say, Mr. Wingfield, please don't let them talk about the organ till I come in, will you? I won't be two shakes: it'll still be light enough to do most of haying and things after tea."

Sula was so surprised at the speed of Lindsey's movements after this that she stood and stared at her for a moment before swinging away into the orchard for her usual routine of drink, roll and shake.

"If you were always as fast as this," said Dion, "think of the extra time you'd gain! It would amount to weeks and weeks, if you kept it up for a lifetime."

"You're just like Holleybone!" said Lindsey, leaning her weight back to balance her pitchfork toppling with hay. "Always talking about saving a couple of minutes. And what does he do with them when he's saved them?"

Tea was quite delicious, For Mrs. Thornton—besides having brushed her hair back—had made all the things she was best at, in honour of having a visitor. But, though the chocolate-cream sponge was Lindsey's favourite cake, and she liked the crunchy brown rolls better than any other kinds of bread, and the yellow butterfly cakes were light as soufflés, she might just as well have been eating turnips, for all the taste she was aware of. There was too much on her mind to allow her to pay much attention to her stomach;

and it wasn't only the delicate question of bartering shooting for organ lessons, it was the news that Freyni's swelling had burst at last, and that she had eaten her first meal worth the name for nearly a week—a saucer of lightly steamed fish.

"All owing to your hot water fomentations," her mother had told her. "Now we'll really see her getting on."

What with the joy over this, and the apprehension over the organ, Lindsey was relieved when tea was over and the grown-ups finally left such subjects as how to deal with the mole-hills on the lawn, and whether roses grown from cuttings were ever really satisfactory, and began in their roundabout way to bring up the question of the organ.

Nothing is ever so bad as you think it is going to be, and nothing is ever so good, so Lindsey had once heard. To her surprise the first part of this theory was quite true, concerning the arrangements for her lessons. Once the tricky subject had been mentioned, by her mother, and taken up by Mr. Wingfield and her father, it seemed only a matter of minutes before all was smoothly settled and she was to go down to the church for lessons every Friday (with the vicar's permission), in return for Mr. Wingfield's shooting over the fields of Punchbowl Farm whenever he could get away from his work to do so. And so the strange bargain had been struck and the subject changed already, for Dion was saying now, "Have you ever heard of a trained gun-cat, sir?"

Lindsey hung around, swaying on her elbows on the sofa-back, listening contentedly to talk of Vashti's prowess with the gun, and then to Peter's tale of Mr. Muncher's awkward character and the difficulties of ever catching him again. She half-hoped that the organ would again be mentioned before she simply had to dash out, with the last glimmer of day-light, to shut up Phasian and the geese, hay the ponies and help Dion with the hens, but it wasn't.

"Perhaps it is just as well," she said to Peter as they followed Dion out into the darkening garden and down through the farmyard. "It would have been awful if he'd suddenly remembered a meeting or a choir-practice or something, and had to put off my lesson."

"If there is one, he'll have to put it off anyhow, by phone or something," said Peter.

Lindsey stopped by the ark where the pheasant-bird lived her lonely life, and Peter watched her companionably while she crept inside the low peak-roofed run.

"She's left a lot of food," he remarked, peering through the wire-netting. "Either she's off it, or you gave her too much."

"Too much, I expect. It's difficult judging how much to give one hen, when you're used to feeding more than two dozen."

"It'll encourage rats. You've only got to divide by two dozen. I say, hasn't she started laying again yet?"

Lindsey had gathered the unresisting bird gently into her hands and was stowing her safely in her night quarters.

"If you'd seen all your friends and relations cruelly slaughtered, and just escaped death yourself, you wouldn't be too keen on starting work again in a hurry."

Shutting the little inner door firmly, she picked up the dish of discarded mash and the half-empty water tin and backed out with them into the yard again.

Down in the cow-shed Dion was already milking. The open door and the dusty windows were full of the warm glow from the hanging lantern, and the high metallic sound of milk-streams hitting the bucket bottom could be heard above the comfortable rattle of Duchess's chain and the far faint tinkle of the heifer's bells in Barn field. Lindsey tipped Phasian's water tin, shaking off the last drips before using it to cover up the food dish.

"I'll pick it up on the way back." She gave a last look into the ark, now almost obscured in gathering darkness. "Well, she's got some oyster-shell, if she does think of laying, and I've done her all over with the cats' flea-powder. You know, Peter, I used not to care very much about hens, but now I begin to think they might be really interesting. Perhaps, if Phasian goes broody, I might ask Dion if I can set her on some eggs."

"What, in October? They only brood in spring. Do come

on, or we'll be haying in total darkness, and I've still got my hamsters to do."

She turned with him towards the barn, now black against the sky.

"Yes, I know of course, now I come to think about it. It does seem a long time."

Then, a little later when they were stuffing hay into hay-nets in a barn as dark as a cavern, she added, "All I'm going to put on my Christmas list this year is hens, skis and a piano. If we get a lot of snow this year it would be marvellous ski-ing in the Punch Bowl."

Peter grunted. "A piano? How many *more* instruments? Not that you'll ever get it."

It was late, and he still had his hamsters to feed and shut up, and his homework to do, and there was the model glider he was making and which he was itching to get on with; but at this rate it would be bedtime before he even looked at it.

Their dark figures showed up in silhouette against the glow of Dion's lantern light as they passed with loaded hay-nets, ready for the school ponies in the morning; and now the milking sound was deep and frothy.

Dion had early discovered what a thought-provoking process milking is; and just now he was thinking about foxes. Not only about Saturday's shoot (in which he had enrolled Mr. Wingfield) but about a scheme for protecting the few remaining poultry from the few remaining foxes, after the Saturday. Duchess was happily chewing her cud, in the odd sideways manner of her kind, and the double rods of milk stabbed down into the thickness of the froth; but Dion hardly noticed these familiar things—partly because they were familiar and partly because he was so pleased with the sheer simplicity of his notion, which was just to leave a lantern, turned down low, beside the poultry arks. Doubtless other people had thought of this before, because it was beautifully obvious, but if they had he had not heard of it. In jungles people lit fires to keep the wild animals away at night. It seemed quite likely that any kind of light would be similarly effective, and though the arks

81

were near the farmhouse now, it was as well to take every precaution; for even old birds past their laying prime, and one quite mental, were worth an effort when they were all you had left to build up with again in the spring.

CHAPTER NINE

Before the Night is Half Over

AT supper in the kitchen that night everyone was very light-hearted. Especially Peter, who had gained nearly half an hour of extra time with his glider, Mrs. Thornton having overlooked his earlier suppertime because she was so involved in patching holes which the cats had made in the sitting-room loose covers.

"I've finished the whole fuselage now," he said, cutting open his jacket-potato, hot from the oven, and pushing yellow slivers of butter down into the floury cracks. "She's really beginning to look something like a flying model."

Dion had caught up with his homework, which was German, and was cheerfully airing it while pouring out cocoa from a large brown jug.

"I can address a German meeting any day now! *Meine liebe Herrschlaften——*"

"Oh, shut up, Dion! You can't imagine how silly it sounds."

"That's nothing, old chap. I used to know 'The political situation, is it a crisis?' but I've forgotten it now. What on earth are you pulling faces for?"

"I'm pretending I'm a cow chewing the cud."

"Well, don't, you can't imagine how silly it looks."

Lindsey took little notice of either of them. She was so absorbed in the—to her—earth-shaking fact that Freyni was actually, audibly purring, on her knee beneath the table, for the first time since her poisoned leg began. Her small ears flickered in their curiously mobile way at every different voice or sound, and her short stumpy tail that Lindsey called her "stalk" was curled as far as it would go across her paws.

It was into this pleasant scene that the bombshell dropped.

"Wasn't that the phone?" Peter suddenly asked, his knife and fork suspended.

Dion said, "Mother and Dad are in there, if it was," and went on with his supper, and with a fascinating game of telling the others just how he would farm the whole place, if money and time were unlimited and school abolished wholly from his life.

"And what about Punch Bowl field?" Lindsey asked, stroking Freyni happily. "You'd find that a sticky problem."

"Oh, I'd have to have a bulldozer for that, with all those overgrown hedges, and the pines and birch and heather all over the place."

"It'd absolutely ruin it," Lindsey was just beginning to say, but at that moment Mr. Thornton appeared in the doorway.

"That was upper Ridgeway Farm on the phone. They've just seen our heifers pass their place, going towards the Punch Bowl."

Lightness passed from the faces round the table as if something had been switched off behind them. They all stared at their father in silent blankness; then Dion suddenly said, "But Lindsey and I blocked every possible place in the hedges, only on Sunday! Was he sure they were ours? They were in Barn field when we came in."

"He said they had bells on."

"And school tomorrow!" said Mrs. Thornton in dismayed tones, coming in with Vashti on her arm. "You've all got to get up early, so you'll just have to get to bed in good time. George and I must go out and find them, that's all."

"Oh, Mother! What nonsense. Dion and I are old enough to stand a late night once in a while," said Lindsey, bolting her last half-potato. "Is Chalice with them too, Dad, did he say?"

"He didn't, but I wouldn't mind guessing that he is," said her father dryly.

"Led them out, of course," said Dion, "the way he always does. You'll have to let us go, you know, Mother. The more

84

people we have out, and in different directions, the more likely we'll be to find them; but if Dad and Lindsey and I go, there won't be any need for you to trudge around, too."

"You can stay by the phone," said Lindsey, who had lifted Freyni on to a chair inside the wide inglenook. "You never know where we might chance to get and want to ring you."

"And you can't leave Peter here alone, in bed, and no dog or anything," said Dion, rummaging in the dresser drawer for gloves and torches.

"I'm always too young for all the fun!" wailed Peter suddenly. "Can't I go too, Mother? Please!"

"Certainly not!" said Mrs. Thornton firmly, feeling rushed enough in other directions without the worry of finding she had let her youngest go out into the precarious jungle of the Punch Bowl and wild valley in the night.

"Besides, there aren't enough torches," said Dion.

"Never mind, old chap," said his father understandingly. "It won't really be much fun when we're out there. You've got the best of it, and we'll all be envying you before the night is half-way over."

"Oh—then we can go!" said Lindsey, dashing for her coat.

"Anyone would think she wanted to go trudging around in the dark," remarked her father, marvelling, as he hunted for his wellingtons among the row upon the door-mat.

"It's not that," said Dion, who knew. "It's just that she's worried about the colt."

"But, George," said his wife anxiously, looking at the clock and at the black expanse of the long diamond-paned window, "don't you think we might, perhaps, leave them till the morning? It looks dreadfully dark, and misty, too. Then we would have daylight on our side; and surely they can't come to much harm, just till then?"

"But, Mother!" said Lindsey, back again with her coat. "There's all the traffic on the main road, and think how far they might get, too, before the morning."

"Probably ruining other people's crops and gardens,"

85

said Dion, his own coat already on and buttoned because it hung behind the door, "which we would have to pay for—even if they don't hurt themselves. Come on, Dad and Lindsey, if you're coming; we're losing time."

"Oh dear," said Mrs. Thornton, trying to think of some way out. "And no one with any watches, except your father. Well, if you do go separate ways, Dion, you and Lindsey must judge an hour as best you can, and come straight home, whether you've found them or not. Even that will make your bedtime far too late, with school tomorrow."

"At least it isn't raining, the way it was last time," said Lindsey, allowing herself to be buttoned up to the throat.

"And we've done our homework," said Dion. "Don't worry, Mother, we'll soon be back; and think what a nice peaceful evening you can have, with the cats and the fireside all to yourself!"

Mrs. Thornton nearly said, "The mending, you mean," but as the three of them were just going out into the darkness she changed it into last-minute anxious reminders about not going too far, not getting cold, not losing their torches (as if they would! thought Lindsey, marking time by the Well House just outside), or Dion's spectacles, and coming straight home, whether or not——

"All right!" said Mr. Thornton soothingly. "Don't worry, dear; we'll all be back in two shakes."

And they were gone.

Mrs. Thornton strained her eyes for a last sight of them, almost as if they'd been bound for the Antarctic, thought Peter, putting down his plate for Vashti; but all she saw was the high dark peak of the little Well House roof against the higher, far darker bulk of the yew tree on the bank, and the gathering mist all around.

Going out through the garden gate into the farmyard, Mr. Thornton said, "Well, what's the plan? Rocky Lane first, I suppose, and up past Ridgeway. We know they went that way."

"Oh, no, Dad," said Dion, noticing that his fox-lantern was burning well by the poultry-arks, "not all of us the same way. I should say one down Rocky Lane, one round

86

by Sandy Lane and one up through the field track, in case the heifers turn back."

"If you're sure neither of you mind a lonely trek in the dark."

"If Lindsey does she can come along with me."

"Of course I don't!" said Lindsey stoutly, hoping the doubt in her mind didn't show in her voice, and telling herself that when her eyes got used to the darkness everything would seem much lighter. "All the same, I'd rather go up the fields, because both the lanes will be as dark as tunnels, with all those branches overhead. And in the fields, you know you're on your own land all the time, and that's sort of comforting."

"You'd better take Sandy Lane then, Dion," said his father, opening the stable door. "Better than Rocky Lane, with your glasses. Then if you meet Lindsey at the top you can both do the Punch Bowl together. I can only see two halters," he added, shining his torch over the oddments of harness on the dusty wooden pegs along the wall.

"I left one over the partition." Lindsey reached for it, suddenly noticing how the dark empty stable was still so crowded with the smell and sense of horses that even if you were blind you would know it was a stable, not a cowshed nor a barn.

In a moment they were out again, in faintly misty moonlight. Mr. Thornton shut the stable door.

"Don't stay out long, either of you; and good hunting!"

As quickly as that, the warm security of companionship had gone, and the loneliness of darkness had closed down on each of them.

Dion took the short cut out to Sandy Lane through Barn field and Hunter's field. The bobbing white scuts of rabbits when he suddenly switched his torch on were a tantalising sight, and set his mind off on possible ways of shooting in the night. The rabbits were always so much more numerous then, and you could get much closer to them. But even the brightest moonlight was not enough to see the sights on your gun quite clearly, or even to be perfectly sure that it was a rabbit you were after, and not someone's cherished

cat. Supposing you strapped a torch—one of the flat kind
—to your belt? But that wouldn't throw any light on the
sights, even if it did shine up the target. Could you tie the
torch—a long one this time—on to the stock of the gun?
Or would that interfere with vision? Perhaps if you took
someone with you, and got them to shine the torch right
over your shoulder, along the barrel—but that wouldn't be
at all the same as having everything under your own control;
and if it was Lindsey she'd hate it, and if it was Peter he'd
talk . . .

Lindsey's way was up the steep track into Yew Tree field,
where she turned for one last glance at the homeliness of
lit-up windows in the farmhouse. From this three-quarter
view she could see three; those of the kitchen, the sitting-
room and the boys' bedroom, glowing warmly in the night.
Then the kitchen one went out. Lindsey turned again and
hurried on towards Lower Naps and the high fields. She
fought a battle with herself about using her torch, if only
for the courage its little beam would give her, but as she
could now see perfectly well without it she couldn't find a
strong enough argument for it. Then suddenly she decided
it was just as well to be without it after all, because a light
would only make her more conspicuous if any nasty
characters were about, and up here on the higher land she
was above the friendly veil of the mist.

The ponies were both in Lower Naps with Duchess, and
Lindsey began to hope for the impossible—that Chalice
would have found his way around to them: impossible,
because there was the whole steeple-sided pitch of the wild
valley between the Ridgeway Farms and Lower Naps, and
it was a long way round by road and track.

The words and music she had written for the colt were
going round and round inside her head:

> O come, my little chestnut colt,
> Do not wander in the night,
> Where the bracken and the gorse
> Hide you from my shadowed sight.

How true it was! And, of course, there was no Chalice,
and no heifers, when she suddenly made out the shapes of

grazing ponies near the path. Just Nanti and Sula, and
Duchess a little apart, as she had really known it would be.
The ponies raised their heads and whinnied, hearing her
steps, and Lindsey answered, a little scared of the sound of
her own voice in so much darkness. The ponies came
towards her, stepping warily, heads moving this way and
that; and then she could see the details in their outlines:
the star on Nanti's brow, the bush of Sula's mane, and the
shining glints of their eyes when they moved their heads.
If she flashed her torch the eyes would be red, like rubies,
but Lindsey resisted the temptation. She hurried on, patting
the ponies for a moment as she passed them; leaving them
reluctantly because, for all she knew, they might be the last
friendly familiar creatures she would see that night until
she reached home again.

Through the shadowy sea-swell of heather in Upper Naps
and Upper Six Acres Lindsey would have run, except for
the steepness of the track and the feeling that she must
listen carefully for the least sound of faint-ringing cow-
bells. But in Nameless field she did run, for here the high
hedge of Punch Bowl field hung close and low above the
track, and the tall dry bracken crowded to the other side,
and there was a hemmed-in feeling, almost as if one might
be drowning in the shadows.

She ran so hard that she didn't hear the footsteps in the
lane, and when she nearly ran into Dion where the high
fields ended she jumped till the nerves in her fingertips
tingled.

"Oh—it's you! Gosh, you did make me jump!"

"Of course it's me. You've been jolly quick coming up
through the fields."

"And I stopped a minute and talked to the ponies,"

"At least they're in their proper field, then." Dion turned
to face Highcomb Bottom and the Punch Bowl. "Coming
with me?"

"Yes," said Lindsey, wishing she had felt indifferent
enough tonight in the Devil's Punch Bowl to say no. "I may
as well now. Which way, do you think?"

"Down towards the gamekeeper's, I should say. They're
pretty sure to come that way, if Dad hasn't overtaken them

—and wasn't that his dog and tame fox barking just as you came up? Then out to the main road, in case they've gone farther than we think."

They covered the distance down to the gamekeeper's cottage much quicker than any similar stretch that night, for it was nearly all sharply downhill and there was a fair path through the heather and bracken, though it was narrow as a sheep-track and slippery with stones, and the mist came up it from the valley.

Mr. Rose, the gamekeeper, had both a dog and a tame fox in kennels in his garden, and both of these set up a sudden racket of barking and yapping as they sensed strangers near the lonely cottage.

"Would they have barked for the heifers?" Dion wondered. "If so, they've probably passed this way already. I'm sure it was these two barking when you came out at the top of Nameless field."

"Mr. Rose is looking out," said Lindsey.

The front door of the old cottage was opening and letting free a stream of misty light upon the path. Like a figure circled with a halo, Mr. Rose stood on the step.

"It's only us—the Thorntons!" Dion called. "Have you seen or heard our colt and heifers, Mr. Rose?"

"What, out again?—*Quiet*, you dogs!—No, I haven't, Dion; but my old dog and vixen started creating, about a half hour back. They don't usually, not for nothing."

Lindsey had switched on her torch and was staring down at the path—a softer, less stony path than were those in Highcomb Bottom and the Punch Bowl—but there was nothing she could be certain were the tracks of Chalice or the heifers. It had not rained much for several days and all the straying animals were small and light in weight.

"I reckon they'll have gone into the Punch Bowl, lad," said Mr. Rose. "But if I see them any time I'll drive them over."

Dion said, "Thank you very much; but I expect we'll find them all right."

Mr. Rose raised a friendly hand and vanished into the warmth and snugness of his cottage. The flood of light on his garden path had gone with the shutting of his door. The barking broke out again as Dion and Lindsey trudged away along the track towards the Punch Bowl, so that if the heifers had been browsing nearby their bells could never have been heard. Dion kept his torch on now, partly because of his eyes and partly because of looking for tracks or freshly-made droppings on the way. But there was nothing they could be sure about. Nothing that seemed so new it could not have been made by the cows from Lower Rockfield, which were daily herded in the Punch Bowl in the immemorial way. They heard no sound that wasn't a normal part of any English night; no faintest far-distant tinkle of a cow-bell, no whinny, or heavy movement in the heather; and there was no answer to their repeated calling.

"We've been out for more than an hour," said Dion, as they stood finally among the shadowed ruins of the old broom-makers' cottages; the fallen walls lay on the grass in scatters of dark stone.

"But we must go as far as the road!"

"No farther than that, then. If we're late home this time we may never be allowed to hunt for them again, on term-time evenings." He was rubbing the mist from his glasses as he spoke.

They went on, through the pathetic brambly patches that had been the cottage gardens, towards the rising southerly side of the Punch Bowl. A bus was gliding round the road upon the high rim of it, its lighted windows above the mist looking strangely civilised in such a lonely wilderness.

"Must be about twenty-past nine," said Lindsey, watching it. "You're right, it's more than an hour."

But Dion wasn't watching the bus. He was staring hard, incredibly, at something very much nearer. Something a thousand times stranger.

"Lindsey!"

His hand was on her arm.

"Yes? . . . Dion! What on earth is it?"

She was staring too, her heart going faster suddenly. They moved a yard or two nearer, their torches spot-lighting the dark shape just ahead: and then there was no mistaking it—the shape was a large saloon car, upside down, near the bottom of the long steep drop from the road, with its four wheels lifted helplessly in air.

A few horrified strides confirmed their rising fear, for their torches lit the quiet form of somebody huddled up inside.

CHAPTER TEN

Beloved Exasperating Wanderer

LINDSEY felt as if she could have run and run with the sheer burden of her fright, and never have stopped until she reached the haven of Punchbowl Farm; but because Dion was with her, and behaving so quietly and sensibly, she took hold of herself as one holds a frightened horse and followed to the wreckage of the car.

"The thing is, the doors will probably be jammed," he was saying, just as if it were daylight and the problem only on paper: but no one could have been more aware than he was of the situation's grimness.

Lindsey said nothing, holding her torch where it might be most use, and praying inside her mind, with the strength of ten, that whoever this stranger was he might not be dead, or very terribly injured. Watching Dion struggling with the door handle, she wondered if she would be able to do anything at all but stand and quaver, if the worst were true. Through the wet glass of the car windows very little could be made out, except the huddle of the figure on the capsized roof, and the steering wheel so crazily stuck up above and hanging downwards.

"Better try the other side," said Dion, going round the car; and Lindsey followed, walking in a nightmare, certain that once Dion got the door open a corpse would fall slithering at their feet. At least it was only one person, she reflected—one could be thankful for that. It might have been a whole family, with people like Dion and herself, all rolling over and over to the bottom of the Punch Bowl, and lying trapped inside the car until she and Dion chanced to pass that way and find them.

"Good gracious!" said Dion. "It opened as easily as

anything. The other was jammed quite tight. I suppose the strain must have caught the other side most."

Lindsey stared at the opening door and wondered how he could possibly speculate so calmly. But Dion knew how steadying is ordinary conversation in moments of emergency, not only to the listener but to the speaker as well; and he was much more shaken than he would have liked Lindsey to know.

"If you could give me a hand, we might be able to straighten the poor fellow out a bit."

"But you shouldn't move anybody after an accident! You might do them more damage still. Supposing there's an internal injury, or something?"

"Yes, I know; but look at him, Lin. If anyone's as huddled up as that it must be much more important to get them comfortable than to leave them where they are. I think I can just get inside—the seats are so awkward hanging downwards—and then if you can lift his legs——"

"Wouldn't it be best to try to get some help first?"

Lindsey sought about for any other way than taking hold of those bunched legs.

"Where from? Mr. Rose's is too far now—so is Hindhead, and nothing's passed along the road since the bus. Come on, Lin; he might die if we don't do anything at all."

Dion was already half-way into the upturned car, cautiously edging himself round to the shoulders of the man.

"Dion—you don't think he's dead already?"

She watched her brother thrust a hand inside the grey tweed overcoat, wondering again how he could do it. Probably he was of the stuff that makes the best doctors, and would be wasted as a farmer after all.

"He's alive all right. I don't know about injuries, with all these clothes on, but he must be pretty knocked about. We don't need to get him out of the car; it'll be warmer inside, and the flat roof's fairly comfortable. We'd probably only hurt him badly if we tried to move him any farther. Just take his legs, Lin, and help me lay him out straighter.

But for Mike's sake be careful, in case he's broken any bones."

Lindsey knelt inside the doorway keeping low, because of the seat-backs hanging above her, and squashing all her instincts for sudden flight. She made herself look at the still face in the light of Dion's torch—squarish, pleasant, a little tanned, the hair very dark; he might be somewhere in his thirties, and seemed peacefully asleep. She curled her hands gingerly under the doubled-up legs, terrified lest they might be broken and move all ways they shouldn't; and as she eased them, one after the other, gently, slowly, into straightness, she was sure they were too limp. Then suddenly a new fear struck her.

"I suppose, if the car were going to burst into flames, it would have done so by now?" she asked a little anxiously. "They do, sometimes, don't they? It's the petrol tank, I think."

Dion was trying to work the fallen cushions of the seats into padding for the head and broad shoulders of the stranger, his torch propped between a book and a parcel lying where they had been flung. He said, "The trouble is that we don't know just when it happened. But they usually explode at once, if they're going to at all. Now, that's much better, Lin; and there's even a rug to put over him—tuck it round your side. He ought to be all right for a bit now, while one of us dashes to get help."

"Must it be just one of us? Dashes where?"

"We must leave someone here, in case he comes round or anything. Well, I suppose Hindhead's the best idea; it's the nearest for the phone—we can phone the hospital and Mother as well—and if anything comes along the road we can stop it and get a lift. Which would you rather do—stay or go?"

"Oh, I'd much rather go!"

Lindsey glanced quickly at the battered car and wondered what it would be like to stay on guard, in mist and darkness, over the silent man inside it.

"Got any money for the phone?"

"Oh—no, I don't think so. But I think you can phone an ambulance without."

95

"Yes, but what about Mother? Look, here's a sixpence; get it changed wherever you can. The shops'll all be shut, but the White Hart will be open, I expect—or any house. And if you can use a phone nearer than the post office one, do. Tell the ambulance to go slowly and sound its horn round the Punch Bowl corner, and I'll flash my torch. And I say, perhaps you'd better ring the police as well. You always have to after an accident, and you can do that without any money, too."

"All right. I'll be as quick as I can."

It was a pity the side of the Punch Bowl was so steep. Lindsey tackled it like a pony on a mountain, but soon she was panting, legs aching, for she was tired already from long walking and the lateness of the hour, and she was forced to go much slower. It was maddening, when she was more than half-way up, to see the lights of a car go swinging round the high curved road—a car that might have carried her to Hindhead, if only she had been earlier or the car a few minutes later. She wondered what it was that had sent the big black saloon rolling down to the bottom. Perhaps the mist, which had sent down others, including a bus, before now, because though it was clear up on the road at the moment, the mists in this region were variable, coming and going without warning. Perhaps it had been another car, which had not stopped to see the results of careless driving in such a frightful place as this was.

Near the top of her climb now, Lindsey stopped a moment because of the searing of strained leg muscles and the pumping of her heart. She flashed her torch to make certain where she was emerging to the road, and, with a sudden jolt, received her second shock that night. In the level beam of torchlight hung a pair of dark-red jewels.

"Chalice!"

The jewels lifted, and the long clear blaze of the colt's face showed unmistakably as he whickered his reply.

Lindsey's mind rushed round and round chaotically in the minute she took to reach him, the beloved, exasperating wanderer. I didn't hear the heifer's bells—and anyway, where are they? Chalice, right out here; and probably by

96

himself—oh, mercy, can he have had anything to do with the accident? And if so, is he hurt as well? Badly, perhaps—oh, not badly, dear God, so that he'd have to be shot—and don't let the man die either, please! Chalice! Come, little colt!—oh, dash, blow and bother, I haven't got my halter! Must've left it in the car——"

Feverishly she tore at the belt of her raincoat. It was attached with a sewn loop to the back, and Lindsey pulled it off with a jerk. Can't be helped now, she thought, I'll have to mend it later. Come, little colt! Come here, Chalice darling!—Oh, help! Now I'll have to take him into Hindhead. Oh, bother, that means I shan't be able to get a lift; and perhaps the man will die because of my delaying—but if I leave Chalice here beside the road, perhaps he'll die, too; he might easily be run down, and I can't tie him up, with only a belt. Oh, dear, why is life for ever such a problem?

Now she had reached him and her hand was slipping over his thick half-upright mane. Oh, blessed relief! He hadn't tried to avoid capture—unless of course that meant he really was injured.

By now, Lindsey was strung up to a dither of nervousness. She was detachedly astonished with herself to find that the hand that held the colt was shaking as she fumbled in her pocket with the other hand for the small apple that was the colt's reward. While he crunched it she felt carefully and quickly along his back legs, in search of wounds she dared not think of. It was too dark to see much. She wanted to fish in her other pocket for her torch and make a thorough examination, but there was the man in the upturned car to think of, and time was gold-dust running through her fingers. To her immense relief she couldn't feel anything wrong with the three legs in her reach, and there was no wound to be felt where she passed her sensitive fingers. The colt seemed well enough and snuffled at her pockets just as if he were in his own farmyard; then he nipped her good and soundly, on the shoulder, just when she was going round to run her hand along his back and down the off hind leg. Steeling herself to do it, Lindsey smacked him on the muzzle. Not very hard, because (quite apart from hating to hit him) she was afraid of losing him again. Chalice jerked his head back, eyeing her sideways, and Lindsey wished again she hadn't been so scatter-brained at the scene of the accident as to leave her halter there; for she had no proper control, especially against nipping, with the belt.

The off-hind seemed sound, too. He lifted it freely as her hand ran down it. Quickly Lindsey straightened up, turned, and led the colt on, trying to buckle the belt as she walked; but her hands were so shaky she couldn't get the spike into its proper hole, so recklessly poked another one.

Once on the road, and the colt going fairly smoothly but in his usual fits and starts, she began to calm down, the nervousness flowing out of her as weariness flowed back.

There was no traffic, nothing at all on the road. Only the colt's pattering bare hoofs and her own dull-thudding wellingtons as her tired feet pushed themselves onwards. She was made more tired by the continual stopping and starting than by the pressing forwards. When she was nearly into Hindhead a lorry passed her, but it was too late to be of any use, even if she hadn't had the colt who backed and snorted, mistrusting headlights, engine noise, hard road, and everything about him. The driver leaned out and stared at her as he passed, but Lindsey was past caring, and had her hands full besides in quietening the colt.

How on earth I'm going to telephone, she thought, as she approached the White Hart Inn; and suddenly it seemed as if her problem was already solved, for the lighted door swung open and out stepped one, two—at least six or seven customers, into the road. It must be closing time, then—oh, help, ten o'clock already?—and surely someone out of all these people could help her in her predicament.

They were in no hurry to go home, it seemed, and hearing the unusual patter of an unshod colt, they turned and watched him come into the bay of pale light from the door and windows of the inn.

"Anything wrong?" someone asked, taking in the belted colt, the tired girl leading him and the look of strain she had.

"Oh, yes!" Lindsey stopped a yard or two away because Chalice snorted, backing, at the lights and strangers.

98

"There's been an accident—a car rolled down into the Punch Bowl. There's a man inside it; my brother's with him, and I've got to phone an ambulance: but now I've got this colt——"

"Bless you, child, hand him over! I'll look after him," a tall man said. "Got any money for the phone?"

"There's been an accident"

He looked more like a farmer than anyone else in the group, Lindsey thankfully noticed, and Chalice was not being really wildly unreasonable.

"It's the light, I think—and the road and everything. If you led him into the side——" she said anxiously. "Oh, yes, I've got sixpence, thank you. You won't let him go, will you?"

"Where is the car?" another man asked as Lindsey cautiously handed Chalice over. "Some of us could go out and see if we can do anything."

"Oh, thank you! It's just about below that nasty corner, where the bus went over; and my brother will flash a torch if you shout. Could you take some hot tea or something, do you think? Or anything you can think of—blankets, perhaps. I'll be as quick as I can," she said to the man with the colt. "If you talk to him I think he'll be all right."

Inside the inn Lindsey was shown to the telephone and her sixpence was firmly refused. "The least we can do . . ."

First the ambulance, she thought, waiting anxiously for exchange to answer. Fortunately for Lindsey, she was particularly good at saying what she meant in a few clear words, not waisting precious time in vagary. The ambulance, with a doctor, was to be dispatched at once, she was told; and with a great sigh of slackened tension (nothing she could do now in personal strain or endeavour could make the least difference to the stranger) she asked exchange for the number of her own home.

"Mother, is that you? This is Lindsey . . . Yes, I know we're terribly late, but it can't be helped . . . and I'm so glad Father's got the heifers; I've got Chalice; fancy him being so far away from the heifers . . . Well, you see, there's been an accident . . . No, not to Dion and me; we're perfectly all right; but we found a car at the bottom of the Punch Bowl . . . Yes, one man . . . Not dead, but unconscious, so I had to come into Hindhead to the phone . . ."

Why was it so difficult to explain to an anxious parent? Lindsey had to spend at least ten minutes over it, and then was unable to prevent her father's setting out again to meet them: and still there was the police station to be telephoned, and the long walk back into the Punch Bowl, and then home. She began to think of sleep—warm, floating, oblivious, heavenly sleep—and had to push the thought away with sudden firmness. Mercifully, the police were as laconically brief and businesslike as ever, and Lindsey hurried back to Chalice, refusing offers of drinks, hot or cold, and pleasant things to eat.

"Thank you so much for holding him! Was he any trouble?"

"Bless you, no!" I'm used to horses, though I do use a tractor these days. Brought up with horses, I was. Nice little colt you've got there, miss, and I know one when I see one."

"Oh, yes, he is! But he's an awful worry. We had to sell his mother—after he was weaned, of course—but he never

100

forgets her and keeps on breaking out to go and find her. And he nips."

"I could have told you that!" grinned the farmer, rubbing his arm. "You want to hit him hard when he does that; did you know? Really hard, I mean. Little smacks'll only make him peevish. And the longer you leave it, the worse he'll get."

Lindsey sighed, slipping her fingers under the belt round Chalice's neck. "I suppose you hit him—just now?"

"Well, miss—as it happens, I didn't." He smiled a little sheepishly. "Not being my colt, you know—and I reckon he's had plenty to shake him up tonight. He wouldn't have been mixed up in that accident now, would he?" The farmer was looking at her shrewdly.

"Why should he? Why— " Lindsey began defensively, and then saw where the farmer was pointing, at the off-side flank of the colt.

"Saw it in the light from the windows. Well, now, there's no need to be saying anything about it, of course, but it's a nasty little gash. Goes deep, you know. You want to get that seen to early in the morning. A few stitches—the vet'll soon fix it for him; but it might go septic if you leave it."

There was a cold feeling somewhere down in Lindsey's stomach as she looked at the ragged cut on Chalice's flank. Not much doubt, now, what had caused the car to run off the road and roll over, over and over, down the steep pitch into the Punch Bowl. Where did they stand now? What did the law say? Would the driver remember, when he recovered, and give evidence against the colt—and, if so, what would happen then?

The cold feeling slowly became a sick feeling, and Lindsey turned the colt towards the road.

"I should put a bit of iodine on that, before you go to bed," the farmer said, as she led the colt from the roadside.

"Yes, I will; and thank you very much for holding him!"

"Oh, that's all right, miss. No trouble at all. And, as I said, there's no need for anyone to say how he came by it, so don't start worrying yourself! But if I were you I'd take a walk round your fences. No good shutting the stable door after the colt has got away, as they say."

101

"Thank you," said Lindsey, feeling unequal to starting a discussion on the colt and the Punchbowl Farm fences. "Thank you very much; and good night!"

If he nips me now, she thought as she led him down the road, it'll be the very last straw.

CHAPTER ELEVEN

Dream of Exhaustion

CHALICE was difficult going back in the darkness round the Punch Bowl; perhaps because he was facing homewards and had had enough of wandering for one night. He pulled at the belt till Lindsey's arm was numb with restraining him. Several times she changed sides in order to rest a wooden-feeling arm, and once, when she had to turn his back to approaching headlights, she thought for a moment she had lost him. At least, he wasn't nipping any more, which was a great relief, because she was almost quite defenceless with no halter on his head.

It was easy to see where the accident was now, for the men from the inn had reached the place and their torches looked like glow-worms down in the mist below her as she slowly circled the high rim to the track. The descent was precarious and exhausting, what with the roughness and steepness of the track, and the thickening mist, and Chalice's erratic pulling and stopping. To think, she said to herself, that she had thought he was getting quite good at being led! Of course, he *had* been fairly good around the farm lately, but out here, in the wildness and the darkness, he was such a handful that you'd almost think he'd never had a lesson.

Somehow, she got to the place near the bottom where the torches flickered mistily around the crashed car, and just as she stumbled the last few yards towards it the horn of the ambulance sounded from the road. Torches flashed in reply, and Lindsey had to swing the colt round from the sight of them, glowing closely in the white mist just ahead.

"Hallo, Lin! That was quick work." Dion's voice was a sudden relief. "And gosh! you've got the colt."

Lindsey turned gratefully to face him, keeping the colt's back to the car. "I found him right on the track—miles from the heifers; Father's got those. Chalice must have galloped away from them. How is the man?"

"He's come round. He doesn't seem to be in much pain; but I suppose that comes later, when the reaction sets in or something." His hand was running over the colt's shoulder. "Chalice seems a bit sweaty."

"Some of it's mist, I expect. He's being awful to lead, and I had to take him right to Hindhead. I left my halter here somewhere. Did you find it?"

"Yes, I'll get it for you. I shouldn't try bringing him too close, with all these lights and people."

"I jolly well won't," said Lindsey fervently, watching her brother vanish into the mist, to reappear in the light from someone's torch, close by the car. Turning, she could see more bobbing will-o'-the-wisps up the hill. That would be the stretcher party coming from the ambulance. Looking at Chalice, who stood now with sides heaving and head hung low, she wondered sadly at the extent of the disaster he had caused. One small colt, so quiet and innocent-looking, and all this! For in her mind there was no doubt that he had been the cause of it.

"Here you are; I'll put it on for you." Dion was back with the halter. "Then I think you ought to start home. It's awfully late for you, and Chalice'll get chilled, standing about wet like that."

"All right; Father's coming to meet me. Dion—did the man say anything about what caused the accident?" Lindsey tried to keep the anxiety from her voice, wondering if her own conclusions were as shoutingly clear to everyone else as they had been to her; but then no one else knew just where she had found the colt, of course.

"No, I don't think so; not to me, anyway. He thanked us for what we were doing—making him comfortable and all that—which I thought was jolly decent for anyone so groggy, and said his name was Scott—Robert Scott. He gave us his address and asked us to phone his sister, because she expects him back in London tonight."

The colt suddenly sighted the bobbing lights of the stretcher party on the hill, and began to dance about again in a fever of renewed nerves and excitement.

104

"Oh, dear!" said Lindsey, thinking about it all as she held on to him. Then, "The car looks an absolute wreck—oh, do stand *still* a moment, Chalice!"

"Yes, but then it's probably insured. The real damage is to Mr. Scott. But it's no good jawing now; you'd better get that colt home. He'll break out in another sweat if he goes on fidgeting like that."

"Yes, I know. I say, Dion," as he turned away to the car, "did I tell you he's got a smallish gash on his off-flank? It might need two or three stitches."

"He has?" Dion turned back, shining his torch along the colt's swinging side, looking carefully. "Hm, wonder how he did that?"

Lindsey said nervously, "You don't think it had anything to do with the car, I suppose?"

"I don't know; difficult to say. Might have, but I shouldn't think so. There are lots of pine-snags about, and he's been a long way. Now get him home, and put some iodine on it."

"Yes, I will, straight away," said Lindsey gratefully, leading him on and circling widely round the car. Her relief at Dion's reassuring attitude about Chalice's probable part in the accident was overwhelming. So much so that it gave Lindsey sudden new strength in her tired muscles, so that feet which had dragged now swung on hopefully towards home.

For all that, she was so exhausted when her father met her on the edge of Highcomb Bottom that he at once took the halter-rope from her hands and offered an arm for her to lean on.

When they reached home at last, long after eleven o'clock, she would gladly have lain down in the stable, rather than walk the last few steps up the yard and into the house. "Nonsense!" said her father cheerily. "*Nil desperandum;* don't stop walking, but just keep on till you reach the door. It's fatal, once you stop. I'll see to the iodine on the cut, and I'll shut him in the stable till the morning, in case we have to get the vet."

"The man at the White Hart said we'd have to have it stitched——" Lindsey began, but by this time she was several steps away from the stable door and she simply dared not stop. Her eyes were on Dion's fox-lantern, which shone like an encouraging half-way mark between the stable and the house, but Lindsey hardly knew when she had passed it.

Once inside the haven of the kitchen she subsided into a sort of contented dream of exhaustion, sticking her aching feet out in front of her as she sat inside the inglenook, clasping Freyni, and floating in a haze of sleepiness and throbbing tired muscles. And all the while her mother was doing things for her as if she'd been a very small child again; putting her pyjamas to warm on the top of the Aga, making her a bowl of steamy bread-and-milk, and easing off her damp outer clothes while she just sat there, dreamily spooning out the hot comforting squares of sugary bread.

She left a good clearing for the cats and went slowly, nodding, up the crooked twisty stairs. In three minutes, when her mother looked in with a finger-shaded torch, she was asleep.

No one had the heart to wake Dion and Lindsey early in the morning. The school was telephoned—"unfortunate accident—unavoidable late night"—and Peter had the doubtful glory of breakfasting all by himself and setting off alone, on Sula, with his homework in his satchel and a diagram of a new idea in rabbit-catchers folded in his pocket where he could study it while riding through the Punch Bowl. You never knew when great ideas might hit you, and there were whole stretches where it was fairly safe to leave old Sula to her own footsure devices.

As things worked out, the elder two were just up in time to be able to hold poor Chalice for the vet while he stitched the cut neatly together, finishing off the job with an anti-tetanus injection.

"You can't be too careful about tetanus, especially when the wound's been open for some hours. Now here is a bottle of stuff I want you to dab on every night and morning. You shouldn't have any trouble, but let me know at once if it doesn't look right. Blessing we're past the fly-season, anyway."

Chalice was very good, not struggling during the stitching, though whenever he flinched a little, Lindsey flinched as well.

"How did he do it, do you know?" the vet asked.

Lindsey said, "We don't really," trying not to look at Dion; but Dion said, "There are lots of places in the valley and Punch Bowl where he could have done worse than that. And of course he might have got mixed up with the car that crashed there last night, but I shouldn't think it's very likely."

Lindsey's heart thumped for one or two beats, but the vet was already telling Dion about the time his own car had once turned over into a ditch, so the danger was satisfactorily by-passed, for the time being at any rate.

Mrs. Thornton, coming down afterwards to see the colt, very soon got round to the one remark her children were expecting and fearing.

"I thought if we had an early lunch you would at least be able to manage afternoon school. There's no point in losing the whole day."

"Oh, but *Mother!*" Lindsey began. "All that way, just for an afternoon! It's only art and netball."

"But I thought you liked drawing." Mrs. Thornton turned round from leaning on the stable door.

"I do, but not going all that way to do it! I can draw at home, and I can draw what I *like* at home."

"What is much more important," Dion said, "I was going to try a new idea on the heifers. A couple of hours or so would just do it. You know those old Geographical Magazines, Mother? Do you know where they are? Because I suddenly remembered, in the bath this morning, seeing some photographs in one of them of cattle wearing short poles slung round their necks. It was in France somewhere, I think, and it said they did it to stop them breaking through the hedges."

"They're in the top of the court-cupboard," said his mother, "but I really don't think——"

"Oh, *Mother!*" said both children in one shocked and disillusioned voice.

"We-ell—perhaps I'll see what Father says." Her voice

107

was doubtful, but it wavered enough to give rise to a war dance on the dung-heap, and she hastened up to the house before finding she had committed herself entirely.

Mr. Thornton, having discovered a great deal about dace in a book from Godalming Library, had made such excellent progress with his work during the morning that he was able to see his children's viewpoint with more than usual sympathy.

"But George, you were always the one—much more than I—who said how much school mattered!"

"I do think it matters. But I like to be reasonable about it. And, well, just for an afternoon—and in such lovely weather as this! Besides, I think Dion's idea about the heifers sounds worth trying. It'll be worth a lot if we can stop this wandering business."

So, after lunch was over, Dion and Lindsey brought the heifers in. Chalice was left out by himself in Barn field, because he was too excitable to take the risk of his wearing pole or hobbles.

"It seems a pity," Dion said, leaning over the open gate while Lindsey drove the heifers through into the yard, "as he's the worst one. Don't let him through! Come on, Midnight! There, that's got them." He swung the gate shut and dropped the hook inside its keeper. The colt leaned his head over, watching the heifers trotting round the barn towards the cowshed.

"He'd only get his hoof behind it, and break his leg or something," Lindsey said. "He was awful when you tried him with the hobbles."

"You can hardly see his stitched place, in all his winter coat."

"What I hope is that it doesn't leave a mark," said Lindsey, following the heifers to the cow-shed. She shut the calf-box door after them and looked over it for a moment at the two of them; fawn-coloured, deer-like; and the heifers stood with front legs straddled out and looked at her. It was an odd thing, being fetched indoors like this, and they wondered over the reason.

"The first thing is to cut a sapling," said Dion, appearing in the doorway with two billhooks. "There are lots in Barn

108

field hedges. They should all come down, really, to make the hedges grow thicker from the roots. That's half our trouble all these years, going up so high instead of thickening at the bottom. I think we'd best take a pole out of that lot in the west side."

In Barn field Chalice trotted after them up to the towering westerly hedge, nosing round them as they picked a sapling, nipping Lindsey sharply as she stood watching Dion swing his billhook.

"You didn't hit him hard enough! That'll only make him nasty-tempered."

"I did! You weren't looking. And I think, sometimes, we're wrong to hit him at all. I think we ought to give him something else to bite—a stick or a broom handle, or something like that. He'll grow to hate us. Look at the way he's bucking away now."

"Mind yourself!" said Dion. "This pole will be down in a minute; I'm nearly through it."

The small tree swayed a little. Two more blows from the billhook sent it leaning, and with a small crack it sank upon its brown-leaved branches in the grass. The colt reared, pawing air, then with a great snort galloped away to the far end of the field where pointed hollies stood between his ground and Hunter's field.

Lindsey took her billhook, bending to help Dion cut the branches from the trunk. It was a small tree, light enough for Dion to lift easily when shorn down to the central pole. He took it under one arm and Lindsey carried the billhooks.

"If you'll go and see if you can find some rope—about four yards, I should think—I'll saw a couple of lengths from this."

Lindsey found a piece in the stable; it might have been a part of some old plough harness, a home-made trace, perhaps. On her way to the workshop with it she let the pheasant-bird out to scratch around for a while, but the beautiful, foolish-minded hen went hurrying with her to the workshop.

"So long as you keep it out of my way," said Dion, glancing at it. He had sawn his two pieces, each about

109

three feet long, and was cutting grooves for the rope with his billhook a foot or so from each end.

"Shall I have a go at this one?" Lindsey began chipping at the second little pole, and Phasian picked up the chippings in her beak and dropped them, clucking happily.

When they went down to the cow-shed with the finished poles and the rope the hen went racing after them, wings flapping to give her extra speed.

Whinberry walked bump into the barn

"Isn't she *faith*ful, Dion? And honestly, you must admit she's awfully handsome, now she's got over feeling so ill and ruffled."

"Handsome is as handsome does: an egg now and then would put her up in my estimation. Besides, she's like most beauties—no brains. You can't have it all ways. Now, hold that rope tight while I cut it in half. That's the way."

Watching how Dion did his pole, Lindsey tied the second piece of rope with neat half-hitches round the grooves that she had chipped in the other pole.

"Now we've only got to try them on."

The heifers bucked and jumped about, shaking their

heads, but when Dion held them in turn, with a halter rope passed round their necks, they were quiet while Lindsey slipped the pole collars over their small horns. The poles hung horizontally across their chests, too wide for any gap in Barn field hedges.

"Too much rope," Dion said. "We'll have to shorten them a bit, or they'll be losing the poles up in the gorse or somewhere."

They made one knot higher up on each rope and tried again.

"That's just about right, I think."

The heifers bucked round the box with heads lowered.

Dion said, "Open the door, Lin, and I'll drive them out. Then we can see what happens when they're in the field."

For a few minutes what happened was the same as in the box. The heifers walked round and round backwards, until Whinberry walked bump into the barn. Then they stood still for a moment while the colt came galloping up and bucked all round them. Suddenly he lost interest and began grazing. Cautiously, the heifers tried grazing, too; found it was quite possible and went on doing it.

"The next time he goes wandering," said Dion, looking at the colt, "I reckon he'll go alone. And we've still got half the afternoon!" he added, realising the joyful fact. "How about helping with some hedging?"

CHAPTER TWELVE

The Truth of It

DURING the next few days Lindsey was increasingly worried. Now that nearly everything else was going all right, she was burdened by growing anxieties over the colt and the Punch Bowl accident; so much so that it spoiled her joy over the approaching organ lesson, over Freyni's rapid recovery, Phasian's touching devotion, and even over the fact that the colt had stayed inside his field since the Wednesday night, and today it was Friday in the morning.

And what a morning, too! It was impossible not to linger a little over dressing, to lean out of her window and stare in a distant dream at the beauty of the golden trees beyond Barn field. And the gossamer webs like spindrift over the grass. And there was the colt, golden coated, matching the trees; and the heifers with him, grazing with those fantastic poles slung round their necks.

But over everything in Lindsey's life at present, the recent accident was casting a fog of growing uneasiness; for there was no doubt at all in her mind that it was Chalice who had caused the shocking affair on the road above the Punch Bowl. And yet, if Dion or any of the others had seriously connected the colt's injury with the crash they had not said much about it; but then of course no one except herself knew just how near the road the colt had been when she found him.

So far as she knew, poor Robert Scott himself had said nothing at all about it, though he had been conscious and doing well in hospital in Guildford since the night of his admittance. To Lindsey the problems were obvious, though anyone less sensitive might not have noticed them at all. If Mr. Scott had risked his own life so gallantly, had wrecked his car and broken both his legs and several ribs, in order to avoid running down the colt, then grateful acknowledgement was plainly necessary. On the other hand, if he had not realised what it was that he was swerving from (perhaps the mist had drifted), mightn't she be placing Chalice deliberately in danger by betraying him to anyone at all? She didn't know just how much danger, or what kind of danger, because she had no idea what attitude the law would take about such a thing. And it would not be easy to find out from anyone else without casting suspicion on the colt. When she had casually asked her father about it he had said he didn't know, but was pretty sure it would not be so much a penalty for the colt as a heavy fine and damages for the colt's owner to pay; which would probably amount to the same thing in the end, he said, since the colt would very likely have to be sold to pay the damages.

From downstairs came the delicious practical smells of toast and coffee and bacon, their tantalising odours drifting from the open kitchen door and past her window.

Lindsey suddenly hurried, reminded of her lateness. School blouse; there was a button off, drat the thing. Cardigan; it really needed washing, but must do another day. And now she remembered that she hadn't sewn on the raincoat belt she had used for catching and leading Chalice on the Wednesday; she must hope it wouldn't rain. Tie; now where on earth was her tie? Things positively walked during the night, as anyone could see, for she had put everything together of course and now here was the tie, beneath a pile of recorder music on a chair. Some people would never have thought of looking there, she said to herself, scrambling it round her neck as she dashed out and down the stairs and into the kitchen.

Breakfast was a rush, for everyone else seemed late this morning, too. There was her father, eating toast and marmalade while he polished his shoes (for today he took his fish drawings up to the publisher in London); there was Peter, just dashing in from a fruitless sally after Mr. Muncher, who had actually been observed looking through the garden hedge ("If he starts coming *in* the garden," said Mr. Thornton firmly, "it will be open war. Either you catch him or I get rid of him, for we simply can't have all the flowers and vegetables eaten."); there was Dion, rushing in with

113

the milk from Duchess and rushing out again to take her up to Lower Naps and bring the ponies back.

Lindsey's problems were forcibly shelved for the time being, as she was caught into the early morning whirl, eating her own breakfast with her homework propped up against the milk jug.

But on the way to school, riding through the heather on grey Sula, and all through the long day at lessons, games, and more lessons, she thought again about the awfulness of Mr. Scott in splints and plaster at the hospital, all for Chalice's sake, and none of the Thorntons doing anything at all except a single telephone inquiry from their father as to how he was progressing.

During algebra, she thought she might perhaps write him a letter. Then, during geography, she decided that this was very risky, because it would be putting down the colt's misdeeds in black and white—possibly to be used in evidence against him. She wondered again what the law would really do about a wandering animal that caused a serious accident on the road. Animal criminology was so difficult to understand. There was no imprisonment, or fining, as with people—unless it happened to the owners— but with sheep-worrying dogs, for instance, there was death by shooting; and the same for horses or cattle who had killed someone. Chalice hadn't killed anyone, thank heaven, but he had so nearly been the direct *cause* of someone's death that Lindsey chilled to think of it. And, what was worse, he could now be called a habitual wanderer, too; liable to cause more accidents at any time of day or night.

Perhaps the law would say, "Either you guarantee to keep him under control, or else——"

When she thought of this, Lindsey was overwhelmingly inclined to let the whole matter alone; she and the unknown farmer-person being the only ones who were certain of the truth of it. But when she thought of Robert Scott, and how the colt's life was owed entirely to him (and at what cost), she knew she would go on being worried in her mind until she had done something about it.

During French it occurred to her that the police would certainly have done some questioning already. In which case, what cause had Mr. Scott given them for his accident? If the real cause—the colt—why had no inquiries been made yet at the farm? You would have thought, she pondered, that someone would have come to look at all the animals to see if any of them bore a scar. The only thing must be that they weren't sure which farm had had animals straying that night, and so were probably still working round to them.

By the end of the long day, Lindsey had decided that she just might possibly be able to bear the suspense for one more week, and, if nothing had happened by then, to bicycle into Guildford on the Saturday and visit the hospital herself in order to set her mind finally at rest. This would mean taking Dion or Peter into her confidence, of course, because she couldn't have faced such a venture alone. Most probably it would have to be Peter, as Dion was usually too absorbed in the farm to want to leave it, and he was prejudiced enough against the colt for all his wanderings with the heifers. But except for this he would easily have been the best person, because sometimes he could seem wise and understanding far beyond his years.

Her mother might have been a very good person to confide in, but the danger there was that she might feel it necessary to talk it over with Lindsey's father; and since he had started his new economy drive about having to sell all but the essential animals, there was no knowing what might cause his judgment to fall on Chalice, who couldn't be really useful for a year or two yet, whatever happened.

With this overwhelming matter finally settled in her mind, Lindsey found herself able to shove it into the background for a while, firmly squashing it whenever it made a reappearance. This was a great thing to accomplish—not to be always listening for the telephone, or a police car at the gate—because there was so much to enjoy, and it seemed terrible to let one's life slip by, never properly enjoying the fun of it, because of always being too inclined to worry over its problems.

That evening, after racing through her poultry feeding, haying and tack-cleaning, she bicycled in the starlight down the long hilly lane to the church for her first organ lesson.

The fact that homework was awaiting her when she got back took nothing from the sheer delight and awe of being associated with such a majestic instrument; though the sense of complete inadequacy she felt was almost enough to paralyse her fingers absolutely.

"It's like that story about the sergeant-major who was marching troops on a cliff-top," she said to Mr. Wingfield, smiling ruefully, "and he couldn't remember the right word to stop them when they were coming to the edge of the cliff. That's just the way I feel now; so much power in my hands, and I don't know how to control it."

"It'll come, it'll come," said Mr. Wingfield serenely. "Now, let us see what you know already. Do you know any little tune to play on this quiet stop? Just to begin to get the feel of it . . ."

When she got back home, bursting into the kitchen and blinking at the lamplight, Lindsey dumped her music on the table where the boys were finishing their homework.

"I say, Dion, did you know how they tune an organ? They bash dents in the pipes, or smooth dents out, according to whether they're sharp or flat."

"He's pulling your leg," said Dion. "Shut up, I'm finishing an essay. I want to get all this lot out of the way tonight, and then have a long weekend. It's the fox shoot tomorrow, too, and I'm getting up early to help them stop the earths in the valley."

"I'll bet you my next ride to school he wasn't pulling my leg. It's the only way you *can* tune an organ. What on earth's your homework, Peter? What's that diagram you're doing?"

"It isn't homework; it's a plan for a thing to catch Muncher. Look, you see this?" He pointed with his pencil on the paper. "That's the old wire netting chick-run Holleybone made last spring. Well, I'm going to prop it up one side on a short stick, like this, and there's a long string on the stick, and there's a cabbage in the run—I'll draw it in—there . . . Now what I do is, I hide behind a bush, holding my end of the string, you see, and then when old Muncher sees the cabbage and goes inside for it I pull the string! The wire box comes down and Mr. Muncher's safe

116

inside it. I say, do you think Dad would really shoot him if he comes into the garden?"

"Oh, gosh, how do I know?" Lindsey said, trying not to start a new feeling of anxiety for Mr. Muncher. "I shouldn't think so; and anyway, worrying can't help."

"You're a nice one to talk," said Dion. "About worrying, I mean."

Lindsey sighed. "Well, I'm not going to worry, now. I'm going to see how much homework I can get done before Mother comes in and says it's supper. Do look at Cat and Freyni! washing each other at the same time; I love the way they do that! Come on, Freyni darling, and keep my lap warm for me."

CHAPTER THIRTEEN

Indian Summer Morning

In her old brown dungarees and soft blue jersey, Lindsey was sitting on the empty coop which was now Phasian's sleeping place, and she was playing her recorder while the pheasant-bird pecked and scratched companionably round her feet.

The glory of this golden October was extending itself in long successions of dream-days, the like of which nobody remembered; and Peter, too, was making the most of the summery Saturday by getting on with the actual making of the rabbit catcher he had so carefully designed. Lindsey watched him trying various lengths and thicknesses of sticks, and testing them for speedy collapse on the pulling of his string. There was a hole to mend in the wire netting; one that had been made by Midnight putting her foot through it one day when careering round the yard.

"Did you know," she was saying, pausing between tunes, "that Phasian belongs all to me now? Father and Dion were going to give her to Mother for cooking, because they said she would never lay again and anyway was mentally unhinged; so I said I thought that was dreadful—if she wasn't laying yet, no one could possibly say it was her fault, and she might always begin some day without any warning. And as to being mental, well, you've only got to look at her. She even knows her name, and she follows me about everywhere, which is more than any of the others ever did; and look how nice natured she is."

Peter suddenly pulled his string, frowning at the length of time it took to lower the box.

"She does look a bit odd when she just walks round in circles," he said, picking up his stick. "Well, look at her now! the way she's staring at her toes. And what about when she pushes her water dish all round the ark with her beak?"

"She may be a little *eccentric*, perhaps," Lindsey conceded doubtfully, "but I don't think so. I think it's just strength of character. I mean, I think she's got more individuality than the others, and so people say she's queer—just the way they always do with really clever people, who do things differently from others. And in any case, she's so beautiful she should be excused doing ordinary things like laying eggs, she's such a pleasure to look at."

Peter made no reply, squatting over his trap in deep study. Lindsey lifted her recorder and put it down again.

"Dion's gone up with the gun," she said, "and he actually took Cat with him. I hope he gets a rabbit—no, two, because Mother will want one, and I think Freyni really ought to be built up, now he's getting better. Anyway, when he comes down again I've promised to help him harrow Inner Wood, where Holleybone ploughed last Thursday, because they want to get the winter oats in it before the weather breaks. I suppose you wouldn't like to help? It makes such a difference to have someone to clear the stones and things from the harrows."

"Well, I might have," said Peter, "but just now I've got to try out this trap in the Old Orchard; and I might need to stay there quite a long time holding the string before Old Muncher comes along and finds it. I thought of taking a book with me, and some sandwiches or something, and not coming back for lunch. After all, it's life or death for Mr. Muncher."

Lindsey leaned forward and offered Phasian a woodlouse on a stone.

"If you do, you'd jolly well better take a thick jersey as well—and a mackintosh to sit on. It may be an Indian Summer but it is October after all, and jolly cold if you're sitting about—especially behind bushes; they're almost always damp and shadowy. *Mother!* What have you done to your hair?"

Mrs. Thornton paused in the garden gateway, a bucketful of ashes in her hand.

"Doesn't it look all right?" She put up a doubtful hand.

"I've just been trying to trim it up a bit, in front of the bathroom mirror; there never seems any time to go into Godalming, somehow."

"Oh, Mother!" Peter joined in, glancing up from his trap. "It's an absolute *sight!*"

Mrs. Thornton moved on into the yard and emptied the bucket of ashes.

"Well, really, it was you people who started it, saying it looked so old-fashioned the way it was. The only thing is, it's so difficult to see properly in a mirror, and the scissors always move the opposite way to the way you think they're going to."

"I think you need to cut a little more off that side," said Lindsey, studying it.

"Oh, no!" said Peter, deeply shocked. "Her ears are showing already. I think it looks awful, and not at all like Mother."

"And that's what I've been doing for half the morning," said their mother, feeling her ears with the hand that didn't have the bucket. "Cutting little bits off here and there to make it level. That's why it got so short. And how I'm going to catch up with all the housework now, I simply can't imagine. I'd no idea it would take so long to do it."

"Well, I do wish you hadn't," Lindsey said regretfully. "I know you did look rather old-fashioned with those long side bits—and it wasn't only me that said so—but I do hope you'll let it grow again, now I've seen how you look without them."

"Oh, dear," said their mother, turning back with the empty bucket, "well, it can't be helped now. I expect it'll look better when I've washed it; and anyway, Lindsey, considering how you cut your own last summer,* I think you can't really say very much about it." She stopped a moment at the gate and added over her shoulder, "Lunch will be about one, if you're going harrowing, and there'll be lemon meringue pie. It's been quite an achievement scraping enough eggs together for it, now we're getting so few."

Peter picked up the Muncher-trap and set off with it towards the Old Orchard.

*Told in *Spirit of Punchbowl Farm.*

"Well, honestly," he was saying as he went, "I think she looks like someone altogether different! It seems a shame."

Lindsey played her recorder for a while, sitting on Phasian's coop and remembering her own hair and the long bright cloud it had been such a little time ago, before she had deliberately sacrificed it,* like Jo in *Little Women*. It was growing more noticeably now, but still looked like a floor-mop past its prime.

When Dion came down from the high fields Lindsey jumped up on to the coop to see if he had had any luck with his shooting; and there was a rabbit dangling from his belt, and Vashti—that old battle-axe!—running beside him and craning her sharp black muzzle up towards the tantalising smell of it. It was a pity there was only one rabbit, but if she was very persuasive she might get a leg of it promised for Freyni's convalescence.

She reached the kitchen just in time to hear Dion saying, "Cripes, Mother! What *have* you done to your hair?"

"Just trimmed it a bit," said his mother, almost apologetically; then with a sudden laugh, "I begin to know what Peter must have felt like when people kept coming round saying did we know there was a tame rabbit in the orchard!"

"Well, I think it would have been better if you *hadn't* trimmed it a bit!" said Dion with a slow grin, untying the rabbit from his belt.

"It's nice of you to be so restrained about it! Peter said it looked a sight, and Lindsey wasn't very flattering. Lovely rabbit, anyway, Dion! I'll take it down into the cellar. Did Cat retrieve it again?"

"She certainly did! Best gun-cat in the universe—and that's probably perfectly true, as I expect she's the only one, anyway. Just a minute while I clean my gun and I'll gut the rabbit for you."

"She must have some of it, then," said Mrs. Thornton admiringly, as she bent to rub Vashti's chin.

Dion had broken the small gun open at the breach and was pushing the long mop-ended cleaner up and down inside the barrel.

*Told in *Spirit of Punchbowl Farm*.

Lindsey said, "Oh, Mother—and some for Freyni, too? You know how she needs building up after her poisoned leg. I say, what's that odd arrangement on the table?"

Dion glanced over his shoulder as he hung up the gun with his father's twelve-bore above the inglenook, and Mrs. Thornton turned to look at the table: a saucepan, a tea-caddy, a soup plate and the kitchen clock, were all built up like a tower in the middle of it.

"Oh, that? I put it there to remind me that the pastry-case for the lemon pie was in the oven."

"How on earth does all that remind you about pastry?"

"Well, it doesn't exactly remind me about pastry," Mrs. Thornton explained, "but when I see all that build-up I wonder why I put it there, of course, and then I remember about the pastry."

"Mother *darling!*" said Lindsey, suddenly grinning.

"Our unique parent!" Dion said, now busy with the rabbit at the sink.

"It's no different from tying a knot in a handkerchief," said their mother. "Better, because you don't always see a handkerchief. And I must say you would have looked well if I'd forgotten the pie entirely while I was concentrating on my hair."

"What Father will say," said Dion suddenly "when he sees it—help! I do wish these cats didn't climb up my back every time I gut a rabbit; their paws are full of knives."

"Never mind, Mother darling!" Lindsey said warmly. "I'll stand up for you! I suffered just the same when I cut mine."

"Thank you, pet; two against the world! But it's no good worrying; what's done is done, and if you don't go harrowing now, there won't be time to do much before lunch."

"And this afternoon's the fox-shoot," Dion said, rinsing his knife under the tap and wiping it quickly. "Here's your rabbit, Mother. Ready, Lin?"

For two hours Lindsey drove the old tractor and harrows round and round the small ploughed field that was called Inner Wood because of the way the wild woods crept up to it, lapping along one side like a golden sea along a small brown shore. At first Dion had stayed with her, sometimes driving, sometimes jumping down to clear the harrows of old bracken roots and stones and bits of ragged turf not buried by the plough. But after a while he went off to examine the length of old wire netting that for years had protected the young corn in the field from the worst depredations of the rabbits.

"Give a shout if you want me," he said. "I'll be somewhere up and down the wire. Must be sure that's all right, and not full of holes, or there won't be a blade of corn left before the spring."

He took a small coil of single wire from inside the tractor, looked into the tool-box for a pair of pliers which he pushed into his pocket, and then swung away down the headland.

Lindsey was used to driving the tractor now, having long since been drawn into nearly every farming operation—even ploughing, when they were working on Lower Six Acres the year before—but she never quite got over the thrill of it. The sense of power in her hands was almost the same as that she had noticed when first confronted with the organ; except that with the tractor she felt the power was in control, and with the organ she had known it wasn't. But the thrill of driving the tractor—standing on the footplate like Boadicea and swinging the whole snorting monster round at the headlands and away up the hill—was the only thing Lindsey did like about it. She disliked the unremitting smoky racket, when, for all it could mean to the deafened driver, no birds need sing, no wind sough among the trees of the valley, and no bells ring on grazing heifers. She didn't care for the violent vibrations, running up her arms from the steering-wheel and up her body from the footplate; and she simply hated the rank smell of clouding exhaust fumes that blew into her face and made her nostrils curl against them. But Dion was not in favour of old-fashioned ways, and no majestic horses would ever work these fields so long as he was there in charge.

It seemed rather silly to think of him, a schoolboy still, as being in charge of Punchbowl Farm; but everyone knew he really was, of course, even though their father signed the forms, agreements, and cheques, and paid for Holleybone; it was more often with Dion that Holleybone discussed the farming operations.

The tractor roared across and across again, over the shadowed ridges of the furrows, the harrows jingling and wriggling behind. The iron lugs on the back wheels of the tractor were churning the brown earth into double-pitted lines, but the broad spiked harrows smoothed and broke and crumbled it, obliterating plough-ridges, wheel-tracks and all. The field was patterned with the alternate strips of furrows and smooth tilth, showing where Lindsey had passed with her fuming monster and the spiky tail behind it. The broad stripes of harrowed land were not always as straight as one could wish, but on such a morning of shining Indian Summer it was hard not to turn from her work sometimes and look at the banked colour of the woods, at Dion stooping to repair the wire netting, and at the far-distant heather hills away across the valley, flanking Kettle-bury. And sometimes (when Lindsey had been very abstracted over such thoughts as, Would Dion really defend the badgers against any threat from the fox-shooters in the afternoon? and, Had Chalice finally given up his urge to wander?) she had not noticed that the harrows were clogged up until the matted roots and stones had dragged a flattened stripe all down the field upon the crumble of her tilth. Then she would pull up the tractor, jump down and race to clear the muddle from among the harrow-spikes, always in a frantic hurry because of an unreasoning nervousness that the tractor might suddenly start again without her.

When Dion came up the headland again she had been harrowing for about an hour and a half, but the small field was still only about half finished.

"Must be nearly lunchtime, I should think," he shouted over the engine's roar, standing to look across the field. "It's coming up beautifully, isn't it? A few more days' dry weather and Holleybone could finish it and get the seed in when he comes on Tuesday. Oh, what an eternal nuisance school is! I could have done it all on Monday."

Lindsey had stopped the tractor by pushing in the throttle, treading hard down on the clutch and slipping the gear into neutral, but the engine still growled, veiling them with its acrid fumes.

"A pity about meals—though I couldn't *possibly* miss mine today. I'm simply ravenous—and there's that marvellous lemon pie—but I could have finished the field in another two hours or less," she said.

Dion frowned a little, pondering.

"You know, I really think it would be worth giving up the fox-shoot to stay and do it myself. The soil's just right."

"But you promised to go with them, and you were looking forward to it! I'd gladly do it myself, only you know how helpless I am when anything goes wrong; and someone always has to start the tractor for me, and turn off everything when I've finished. And what about if she stalls?"

Dion thought again, his foot resting on the hub of the wheel.

"Well, look, Lin; supposing you have a shot at it—I'll get you started before I go—and if anything does go wrong, just stop her the way you've done now, and leave her till I get back. We'll just cross fingers and hope that nothing does go wrong. But even if it does, you might have covered quite a lot of ground first. I'll show you how to switch the engine and the fuel off, just in case you can remember——"

"But I won't," sighed Lindsey. "I never can, with anything mechanical. It's my limit to remember the gears and clutch and throttle—and even with them I sometimes have to think. If only we had a horse-team, now . . ."

"Well, we haven't. And if we had you'd find them a lot more difficult than you think. Anyway, since you're carrying on this afternoon we'll leave the tractor here ready, so hop down and watch me stop the engine. First turn the fuel off here, at the sediment bulb; then we have to let the engine run slowly till it nearly stops for shortage of fuel; then turn over to petrol like this, just for two minutes."

They stood watching it, Lindsey trying to memorise the details while Dion explained about a thing called a manifold, which muddled her completely.

"Now you turn it right off, like this," he said.

The tractor gave a cough, a splutter and a sigh, and

suddenly there was the most profound silence—or that was what it felt like after so much roaring and racket.

"And then you switch off the ignition, in here, with this lever—like this."

Lindsey said, "Yes, I think I understand. My ears feel funny; sort of singing, now the engine's stopped. And isn't it nice to be able to breathe deeply again? Why don't they have a very tall exhaust-pipe to carry the fumes above the driver altogether?"

"Oh, I don't know," said Dion. "I suppose because most tractor drivers don't mind particularly, and perhaps because of catching in low branches. Now, d'you think you can remember how to do it?"

"I don't suppose so," said Lindsey frankly. "I think the best thing for me to do when I've finished—if I don't get into trouble before—is to drive her down to the yard and just stop her and wait till you come back. Or if Father's home he might come out and turn everything off."

"Much better not to interrupt him if he's working," said Dion. "Anyway, come along; I'm sure that's Mother ringing the bell, and the men will be here for the shoot soon after two."

CHAPTER FOURTEEN

Hostage on a Chain

MRS. THORNTON had not allowed Peter to go on sitting behind the brambles with the rabbit-trap string during lunchtime, but had sent Dion to fetch him back for a proper hot meal, and because she thought he must be getting chilled. He had not had any luck, though Mr. Muncher had skirmished past a time or two, glancing with acute suspicion at the propped-up box, but with (so Peter said) a watering mouth at the cabbage.

"I've only got to keep it up a bit longer to wear him down and then I'll get him—you see. I'm putting some carrots with the greens this afternoon."

As soon as he had dried the knives and forks for Lindsey he was back at his position again, with carrots in the box, but this time he was buttoned into his garden coat because his mother said it soon got colder after midday, now they were so close to winter.

Lindsey hung up the dish-mop, rushed to get her thick jacket and went out with Dion again, up into Inner Wood. A pair of magpies flew up from the furrows as they turned into the little field, and Dion laughed.

"Two for mirth! Looks as if you're going to have a jolly time."

"Much more likely *they* are," said Lindsey, "after the seed is in."

Dion said, walking up to the tractor, "I don't think they're the trouble on seeds; it's rooks and crows. You know what the old sowers used to say? It's on the calendar for this month—'One to die and one to grow; one for the rook and one for the crow.' I suppose they always sowed four times as much as the land really needed. Going to watch me start her up?"

127

"I might as well," said Lindsey, "but it doesn't mean a thing: I just haven't that sort of brain."

"You never know," said Dion. "After all, you've learned the other controls, and now you drive her very well. One day you'll probably be lying under her in your dungarees and doing a job of engineering."

"That will be the day you turn Punch Bowl field into a sanctuary for the deer and rabbits!" said Lindsey with a dry small grin.

When Dion left her a few minutes later she was roaring and lurching across the field with the harrows jiggling and yawing in her wake. That looked all right, he said to himself, watching her for a moment, and then he turned and walked quickly back towards the farmhouse. Everything looked all right; nice weather for seeds, the harrowing was going on without him, colt and heifers in their field; lovely weather for shooting, too, if only the sun didn't dazzle too much on his glasses; and if they got a fox he'd ask to have its skin, and give it to his mother for some gloves: Mr. Morton had said they'd buried the last two they had shot, and it seemed an awful waste.

Down at the farmhouse there was no sign yet of the gathering of the fox-shoot, and Dion filled in the time with racing round and doing all the last-minute things that always crop up whenever a farmer plans to have an afternoon away.

The water for the geese; he was almost sure he had forgotten to fill it up, in all the rush of taking Vashti shooting and then getting Lindsey started on the harrowing. He carried a brimming bucketful into the Little Orchard for them, pouring it into the old kitchen sink which was both bath and drinking-place for the three geese and their gander. The old gander hissed at him and lunged a menacing beak, but Dion grabbed him round his snaking neck, walked him round and round a couple of times as if in some fantastic waltz, and left him facing the other way, dizzily vague about where he was and why.

Then one last glance up Barn field to make sure the colt and heifers were still there. He couldn't see them, but from the faint musical tinkle of the cow-bells he knew that the heifers, at least, were hidden in the gorse and silver birches

128

on the steep far side of the field: and now they wouldn't find it very easy to get through the hedges again.

Then what about Vashti? It would never do to have her follow on a fox-shoot, with guns and dogs on every side. All her training would be ruined. Rushing in at the back door Dion called out, "Mother! Do hang on to Cat whatever happens! You'd better shut all doors and windows, as well as keep your eye on all the chimneys!"

Mrs. Thornton appeared from the larder, where she had been speculating on what to make for tea.

"All right, dear, I'll do my best. You will take care of yourself, won't you, Dion? I don't know, but it seems you can hardly ever pick up a newspaper these days without reading about another shooting accident, usually to a boy."

"Oh, I'll be all right; I'm much too careful ever to have an accident—honestly, Mother." It hardly seemed a good moment to say the next thing he had thought of, but Dion tried it. "I say, Mother, you don't suppose Dad would let me take his twelve-bore, do you? Just for this afternoon? He hardly ever uses it, and no one else will have a four-ten, excepting me."

"Even if he would," said Mrs. Thornton, "I'm afraid I wouldn't. Sorry, Dion old chap, but that's all there is to it —for this year, anyway. And what about your glasses? We will never get your eyes right if you don't wear them, and in any case you won't see properly to shoot without them."

"I know." He pulled the case from his pocket. "The trouble is, it's sometimes just as hopeless with as without them, the way the sun slants on the lenses . . . Wasn't that the yard gate?"

Quickly he reached the cartridge box down from the top of the dresser, filling his pockets. He lifted the small gun out of its leather loops above the inglenook, grabbed Vashti, who leaped from the Aga at the sight of it, and thrust her at his mother.

"Don't let her out for at least an hour, will you? Poor Vashti! It's awful disappointing her, but it can't be helped. Is Father working? Bother, he was going to ask about the badgers, but I suppose we mustn't interrupt him. Don't

129

E

wait tea because I'll have to milk as soon as I get in—and don't *worry!* I'll be all right."

Going down into the yard Dion quickly saw, with some surprise, that he was not the youngest member of the shoot. There were two boys in the yard among the men who were at least a head shorter than himself, although neither carried a gun. They were not much older than Peter, he decided, and suddenly thought that Peter might have liked to come, too; but walking up the steep track into Yew Tree field with the others, Dion saw his younger brother's head behind the brambles down in the Old Orchard, and in front of the brambles was the Muncher-trap, still propped and still vacant.

In Lower Naps the party split; the guns down-wind across the fields towards the Punch Bowl, the beaters out through Inner Wood to drop into the valley by the ford. Now Dion was easily the youngest, trudging up the fields with six seasoned countrymen, their dogs and double-barrelled guns, for the two young boys had gone into the valley with the beaters. The dogs were beautifully trained, following quietly at heel, and Dion regretted silently the dog they used to have at the farm who had died of hard-pad distemper. A gun-cat was a unique and remarkable thing, but there were times, such as now, when nothing but a dog was any use.

At the top of Nameless field they turned sharply, round the edge of Punch Bowl field, and one man left the party and went to take his stand in the high fox-coloured bracken of this long-derelict outpost of the farm. Another, Mr. Wingfield, left them at the valley's brink, and three men, two dogs and Dion went down the plunging drop into the jungle of the valley. Half-way down, Dion was left, and here he loaded his gun and stood for what seemed a timeless period among the spinning-down of red leaves and the drunk-dreamy smell of English autumns. Funny thing, he thought, how easily a man can melt right out of sight in thickly-wooded country; here I am, with six men and four dogs all somewhere within earshot, and I can't see so much as a hint of any one of them—nor of anyone else neither, for no one else would come to such a place, at such a time.

He was on edge, alert for sound of fox or beaters, or for sight of red-brown streak among the tree trunks; so much alert that everything else was noticed too, with sudden clearness. Small Brook hurrying down in the valley bottom; sweet chestnuts, fiercely prickly, underfoot; strange fungi, poisonously brilliant.

The earths in the valley were all stopped. There was no place for a fox to go, unless it was into the setts of the badgers, which he had not allowed the earth-stoppers to touch. Thinking of badgers made him remember Lindsey and the way she was about these things. Queer, how two people in the same family could look at life so differently, though he rather agreed with her about the badgers. But the rabbits, foxes and deer . . .

Jerked from this track of thought by the sound of a shot away above him on the farther brow of the valley, he almost missed the sight of a big dog-fox darting up the nearer bank towards Punch Bowl field. It was well out of range for his gun, but drew fire from Mr. Wingfield, who missed with both barrels but succeeded in turning it sharply back into the valley. Dion, almost too excited to think, raised his gun and swung it along the line the fox was taking, for unless it swerved a second time it must now pass well inside his range.

This was when a curious thing happened, for the fox stopped in its tracks at full speed, with a jerk that threw its head up and sent small stones rattling down to Small Brook. Still holding the fox in his gun sights, Dion stared at it in puzzled astonishment, then suddenly lowered his gun and ran towards it; for he had seen what held it crouching there —the sun, piercing through thick foliage, drew sparkles from the nickel links of a dog-chain.

All in the same moment the fox was seen by Mr. Morton in the valley bottom. A second shot cracked out as Dion came half-running, half-scrambling from the steep jungle into the open. He knew at once from the sharp needle-stabs in his thigh that he had caught the outer scatter of pellets from the shot, and that it was his fault for running out towards the fox. He had slowed a little, holding a cautious hand above his knee, but the pellets did not hurt much.

131

Mr. Morton was shouting and hurrying, puffing as he pounded up the valley side, grabbing saplings and tree roots to haul himself over tricky places.

"What the so-and-so you want to dash out like that for? You hurt, boy?"

"Not much; only a few pellets, I think. I'm awfully sorry, but when I saw the chain I just ran without thinking."

"Chain, what chain? Asking for trouble, I suppose, taking boys out shooting. Lucky to be alive, you are. Got it in the leg, Wingfield," he called, as the choir-master came crashing down the valley side. "Better get him home—and what his mother and dad'll say——"

"But it isn't even bleeding! It's nothing at all," Dion protested. "The fox was tangled in a chain; he's just among this willow-herb——"

"You sit right down, my lad, and let's clap eyes on that leg!" commanded Mr. Morton, as Dion scrambled on through crowding undergrowth.

"I've got a fairly clean handkerchief," said Mr. Wingfield.

Dion said, "I don't need one—look, the fox is here! I think the chain is caught between those stones."

"Don't you touch it, Dion!" The farmer came blowing up to the willow-herb, his gun at the ready. "You'll get your hand bitten off. Stand back and I'll—sakes alive! if that isn't old Rose's dog-fox—the one he had before the one he took after this one got away. Chain and all!"

"Six months ago or more, that was," said Mr. Wingfield. "You'd think he'd look thinner than he does, with that chain hampering his hunting all this time."

"I thought he must belong to someone," Dion said. "That's why I didn't shoot."

"Sensible enough," said Mr. Wingfield.

"A pity you didn't have sense enough not to run out, all the same," said Mr. Morton. "Now, what in heaven are we going to do with the creature? Looks as if it's got a tidy peppering in that near fore-leg. Better finish it, perhaps?"

"Not without asking Rose about it, surely?"

"Oh, well—perhaps you're right. It looks well and firmly tethered at the moment. Dion, let's have a look at that leg of yours. Funny thing, shot. You never know where it has fetched up."

"Knew a man once," said Mr. Wingfield, "who had thirty pellets in his arm. Looked like a blue rash, but he said they never inconvenienced him. Had 'em for years, he said."

Dion was rolling up his trouser leg.

"You said there was no bleeding," Mr. Morton said, bending for close scrutiny.

"Practically nothing," Dion said. "Well, look at it!"

"Lucky thing it wasn't your face, is all I can say. Hurt much?"

"No, not more than if someone stuck some pins in. No need to go home or anything. The beaters will be coming up soon, and then there's the copse by Nameless field." He was unrolling the trouser leg again.

"Home you go, young man," said Mr. Morton firmly. "I'm not going to have it said I trailed you round the countryside with a leg full of shot, nor am I. And you see you show that leg to your mum the moment you get in, for as I say, you never know with shot."

"Oh, but——" Dion began, then seeing the determined look on both men's faces, "but what about the fox? It's hurt as well as I."

"Be all right till Rose comes out and gets it. We'll let him know before it gets too dark."

Less than fifteen minutes ago Dion had been thinking how it was that he and Lindsey were so different. Now, with surprising swiftness, the gap of difference grew narrower. Almost, he began to understand her wide pity for the creatures called vermin by the farmers. But, of course, this fox was rather different, he reasoned to himself, trying to excuse his seeming lapse; it had been the same as a dog to Mr. Rose, it was hurt, and was caught fast with a chain.

Suddenly he said, "I'll take it home with me. Lindsey will be glad to dress the paw, and Mr. Rose can fetch it when he likes. Or we can take it over to his place, when it walks all right. I don't think we ought to leave it here; its paw's in rather a mess."

In the near distance the noise of men trudging through the

heavy growth of the valley told the guns of the beaters' approach.

"Do as you like, of course," said Mr. Morton, "but my advice is, don't. It's likely wild enough again by now to go for you if you have any dealings with it."

"Especially with a wounded paw," said Mr. Wingfield.

"I'll see what happens when I get nearer," Dion said, picking up his gun.

"Well, whatever else you do, don't let it go again," said Mr. Morton. "What this shoot is for is to put these vermin down, not to encourage them. And I should have thought, after all those bullets you just lost, that you'd be the last to go Red-Crossing after foxes."

Dion said, "Yes, it does seem silly, doesn't it? But after all, it is Mr. Rose's fox, I suppose. Not like a wild one at all. And since I have to go back anyhow, it seems quite reasonable to take the fox, too. That first shot," he added, slipping the unused cartridge from his gun, "that wasn't you, was it? It sounded farther away, I thought."

"Not me. That was our Reg. And we better hope he got the vixen, for if we go on the way we're doing now we shan't get nowhere."

Mr. Wingfield had taken off a rubber boot and was shaking bits of twig out from inside it.

"Oh, not so black as all that, Morton. The fox'll be out of the valley, anyway, and if your Reg got the vixen that's two already that won't kill any more chickens."

He was leaning against a beech trunk, one stockinged foot curled round upon the other booted one. The dog-fox licked his paw and kept his eyes upon the three who held his future in their hands.

Dion began to walk towards it, saying, "Good fox! Quiet, then, good fox!" because of course one shouldn't approach a strange animal in silence, and that seemed as good a thing as any to say to a fox.

"Put your gun down, Dion," advised Mr. Wingfield, shoving his foot back into his boot. "It makes for suspicion."

Dion dropped it against a silver birch. The fox stopped licking his paw and watched the boy's approach with wary

134

interest. For a few moments Dion felt little waves of panic trying to take control and turn him back, for a fox-bite could cause the loss of a hand. Then suddenly the pricked ears were lowered softly on the head, the way a dog's ears will, and it was like the lowering of a sword. Confidently now, he took the last step towards the captive, laying a steadying hand upon the chain. If only he had known the name that Mr. Rose had called this fox!

"Good fox!" he said. "Quiet now, good fox!"

Confidently now, he took the last step towards the captive

The fox reached his head away from the strange hand on his chain, but even Mr. Morton could see now that Dion was in no danger.

"The chain's jammed pretty tightly," Dion said, working at it with his hands. The fox leaned out, away from him, its sharp muzzle stretched along the ground towards the valley. "That's got it! Gosh, I hope it can walk all right."

"You better hope it's willing to, what's more," said Mr. Morton. "You won't fancy yourself dragging a full-grown fox along through all those fields, with your own leg full of shot an' all. Here comes the beaters, Wingfield. And there's our Reg. Got the vixen, too! Good lad, Reg! Thought you'd have 'er."

The fox was willing. He could only walk on three legs, but after the first frightened struggle he was more than willing to do so. Mr. Rose had trained him well, and his good training had stuck. Taking advantage of it, Dion picked up his gun and hurried up the valley, plodding gamely though his ley was stiff and throbbing now. All he wanted was to escape before the tale was told to the beaters and the guns across the valley—his crazy running-out, his shot leg, his perverse insistence upon saving the fox, and now his taking it home. All quite uncharacteristic of him, he well knew. He could almost hear Mr. Morton's voice explaining:

"I never knew he were that sort of lad, he always seemed so sensible-like, but there—there's nothing queerer than folks. Think you know them, and they go and do just the plain opposite you'd have wagered. Same with animals. I knew a horse once, nice gentle horse he was . . ."

Hauling himself up the valley-side with every offered hand-hold, disregarding the nagging of his leg, he didn't stop to look again at the fox that limped three-legged at his heels. Only occasionally did the animal pull back with a sudden wild panic that made him fling his weight into his collar, staring valleywards. But up on the high loneliness of Punch Bowl field Dion stopped and shifted the weight from his leg for a minute or so, and looked at his hostage on its chain. The dog-fox lowered his ears and pulled away, but Dion bent and patted the thin shoulder. Under the lame paw the moss was red. This wouldn't do; they had better get home, two wounded creatures as they were. Walking on, he remembered the fox-skin; they had expected he might bring back a skin for making gloves. Well, so he was; but they had hardly guessed there'd be a fox inside it.

CHAPTER FIFTEEN

Quite Enough Trouble

THERE was so much interest and excitement at the farm-house when the wounded fox came home that Dion's own leg was not mentioned for some time.

"But, Dion, whatever made you bring it *here*?" his mother asked, as she and Lindsey struggled with two spitfire cats whose tails were bottle-brushes, contriving to shut them in the kitchen, where they jumped upon the window-sills and swore through the glass.

Dion was sitting on the wheelbarrow and the fox had gone to earth beneath it, only the white tip of his heavy brush showing on the cobbles outside the back door.

"Whose is it, do you know?" Lindsey asked. "I say, its paw is hurt quite badly! Did somebody shoot it? Would it let me look at the place and bathe it?"

"I think——" Dion began, and then his father came round the corner of the house with a dutch hoe and a trowel.

"What on earth——?"

"It's a fox, George; Dion brought it home. And whatever you do, don't let those cats out, will you?"

"Fox? Thought they were going shooting them. Big one too. What are you going to do with it?"

"It's Mr. Rose's," Dion said. "We found it in the valley."

"Then why didn't you take it to Mr. Rose's cottage?"

"Because I had to come home, anyhow. I——"

"No luck at all," said Peter, coming round the corner suddenly with the Muncher-trap in his arms. "He simply wouldn't *look* at all my lovely vegetables after he saw where I was hiding, and now—I *say!*" he said, stopping dead and staring at the barrow. "What on earth is under there? Did you shoot it, Dion? Why is it under the wheel-barrow?"

"If I could only get a word in edgeways, I could explain all about it. I brought it home to look after it till Mr. Rose can fetch it, because I had to come back anyway; I got a bit of shot in my right leg and Mr. Morton said straight home —though it wasn't really as bad as all that."

"Why ever didn't you say so before?" Mrs. Thornton was at once full of anxiety, expecting the worst, and certain that Dion was glossing things over, having probably lost pints of blood and struggled home with the aid of a badly-twisted tourniquet. "Come along in at once—never mind the fox; Lindsey and Peter'll shut it up somewhere— George, give him a shoulder, will you, and get him to the sofa. I'll put the kettle on and then come and have a look at him, and you can phone the doctor."

"Yes, but the thing is," said Peter cautiously, "does it bite?"

Dion said, "It didn't bite me. No, thanks, Dad I can manage. And I don't need the kettle or the sofa or the doctor. All I want is a little healthy neglect; and Lindsey —how did the harrowing go? Any trouble with the tractor?"

"Not a thing," said Lindsey. "I brought her down, and when Dad came out to do some hoeing he turned everything off for me. The field looks simply lovely. Shall we try the fox with some water to drink? D'you know what Mr. Rose called him? It must be the one he used to have, the one he said he lost last spring. Peter, can you find the Dettol?—I think it's in the bathroom—and I'll get the water for drinking and washing."

"I should hitch him up in the Well House," Dion said, giving her the end of the dog-chain. "And don't let the cats out for a bit."

"You come inside at once, my lad," said his father, taking his elbow. "You can't expect us to take your wounds as lightly as all this until we've had a look at them."

"They didn't touch the badgers, did they, Dion?" Lindsey called after him, holding the chain at arm's length.

"No, and when I left them they were going to Nameless field copse."

"Oh, good!"

Filled with sudden gratitude because of the safety of the badgers, Lindsey made reckless vows to herself about helping much more on the farm and never saying again how much she wished the stinking, noisy tractor were a team of gracious horses. She turned to the fox beneath the barrow.

"Hallo, fox! Good fox, come on then!"

Anxiously, she gave a gentle pull upon the chain; but the fox pulled the other way, scrambling farther under the wheelbarrow. Now his sharp black muzzle showed beside the wooden wheel, and Lindsey stood there doubtfully, wishing Peter would come back, or that she knew more about the character of foxes. Perhaps it would be better not to disturb him any more than they could help; she might try fastening the chain to the wheelbarrow handle while she went to get the water, and then the fox could stay where he was.

This idea worked very well until she opened the kitchen door, when both cats came rushing through her legs with growls and bristling hackles. Immediately there was such a commotion that it was heard right through in the sitting-room, and Dion and his mother and father arrived at the door in time to see the wheel-barrow bucketing down the garden path towards the Old Orchard, the lame fox hauling it with more vigour than one might have expected even in a four-legged animal of that size. Lindsey tore after it, with the cats following in stiff sideways bounces, on legs and claws spread out like falcons' feet. Dion rushed after Lindsey, and Mr. and Mrs. Thornton rushed after the cats. Peter, appearing at last with the Dettol, rushed after everyone else, and suddenly the wheelbarrow hit the garden gate with a loud crash and stopped there, the fox on one side and the barrow on the other. Mr. Thornton caught up with Freyni and grabbed her, and Peter fielded Vashti from a rhododendron bush.

"Here you are, Mother; you'd better have her."

His mother grasped her furious Siamese cat. "Dion, go back in the house at once; we can manage."

"Mother *darling*!" said Dion, exasperated. "What a moment to suggest it! I'm not an invalid—you grab the chain, Lindsey, and I'll try to undo your hitches—lots of people go around with their arms and legs full of shot, and never do anything about it—gosh! it *has* pulled tight. Peter, can you get me a screwdriver, or a skewer or something?"

"I think if the cats were shut up into somebody's bedroom it might help," said Lindsey, trying not to feel on edge. "This fox is simply terrified. I don't suppose he's ever seen a Siamese cat before—let alone two, and as hostile as these are."

"I'll take them in," said her mother. "Give me Freyni, George. Oh, dear, I expect the kettle's boiling dry, and we haven't properly looked at Dion's leg . . ."

"Don't worry, old girl; Dion's all right. I'll run him into the casualty place at Guildford hospital as soon as we've sorted out this muddle. I can get that naptha stuff you wanted for the moles while we're in Guildford, too."

"How you can think of such a thing, *now*," said Mrs. Thornton, shocked. "Still, I suppose it'll be just as well to have it; the lawn's in such a state. Don't be long, will you? Are you sure you've got enough petrol? You haven't used the car for days."

"That's no reason for running out of petrol, Mary dear —rather the reverse. Now, do get those cats out of sight, or we'll be here till doomsday."

Peter came rushing down the path again.

"I couldn't find a skewer or the screwdriver, but here's the kitchen scissors."

"Some hope!" groaned Dion. "But give them to me, we can at least try."

"Damage," said Mr. Thornton, checking over it: "Two broken wheelbarrow legs, one splintered gate strut, and a lilac branch. What your mother will say when she sees that . . . Anyway, the fox looks much the same. I shouldn't try stroking it, Lindsey, until it gets over the shock a bit. When did you say Rose was calling for it, Dion?"

"I didn't. Mr. Morton said he'll tell him this afternoon. I suppose he might come any time after that. Can you ease the chain a bit, Lin?"

"I shan't be sorry to see him," said his father, turning back up the path. "Can you be ready in about ten minutes, if I get out the car?"

"Oh, Dad!" said Peter suddenly, "not till I've got my hamsters out, please! I just put them both inside it this morning while I mended a hole in their cage, and then I forgot to mend the hole because of making the trap for Mr. Muncher."

"I will *not* have hamsters in my car!" said his father, very annoyed. "What this family will come to next—rabbits in the garden, foxes careering round with wheelbarrows, ferrets in the sitting-room——"

"That was last summer," said Peter.

"I know it was—and now hamsters in my car."

"It was the only safe place," Peter pleaded. "I'll go and get them now."

"That's got it!" said Dion, levering with the scissors' point. "Now, you hang on to the fox, Lin—here's the chain —and I'll heave the barrow from the gateway. All right, Dad, I'll be ready in a minute. I've only got to put a jacket on."

"Let me give you a hand with that barrow, then; we'll need to lift it if the wheel's as loose as it looks. If I were you, Lindsey, I'd put the fox in Glen's old kennel; he won't be able to race around with that quite so easily. Ready, Dion? Just lift it off the path, we'll move it later."

"Will the fox lead all right, Dion?" asked Lindsey, looking at it anxiously.

"He led all right with me. All he needs is quiet handling."

"Quiet!" said Lindsey feelingly. "What a hope I've got, then!"

But fifteen minutes later, when the car had departed for Guildford with Dion and his father—Peter going too, for the fun of it—and the cats were safely shut in Lindsey's bedroom, she and her mother found the problem of the fox much easier than they had dared to expect. He had allowed Lindsey to lead him, in fits and starts, round to the kitchen door again, but he would not, under any circumstances, go into the house.

"Well, we'll just have to do his paw out here," said Mrs. Thornton. "I've got enough boiled water left from bathing Dion's leg. I'll get it if you'll hold the fox."

Lindsey sat down on an upturned bucket by the door,

141

holding the chain—wrapped round her hand for safety—
and staring at the fox with a mixture of pity, wariness and
puzzlement.

"This is quite the last thing I'd ever have expected Dion
to do," she said as her mother came out with the water in
a basin.

"Just what I was thinking. However, on the principle
that there must be some good in all things, I'm hoping Dion
will now find he simply has to rest more for a while, with
that leg. He really never rests enough, for his eye condition.
Now *where* did Peter put that Dettol? Oh, well, we can use
bicarbonate of soda."

"And what about some cold water for him to drink?"

"I'll get that, too. Then you can bathe his paw while I
have a look at the old kennel. Quite likely we shall find
Peter's got some mice in it or something."

The fox would not drink, but he allowed Lindsey to
bathe the wounded paw without much struggling. Once or
twice she got the paw right under the warm water, which
did good to the places her cotton-wool swab couldn't reach,
and when she had finished and the paw was cleaned of dried
blood and dust she was able to see fairly well the extent of
the damage.

"I don't think it's really very bad," she said as her mother
passed with a piece of clean sacking for the kennel. "It
doesn't look as if anything's broken, and it's not bleeding
much, any more. Will you come and have a look?"

Mrs. Thornton bent over the paw and examined it, the
fox shrinking farther away into his collar.

"No, not bad at all. But my word, doesn't he smell!"

"Oh, only foxy. Shall we bandage it?"

"Yes, I think we'd better. I'll get some old sheeting I've
been saving; it'll keep it clean, anyway. I wonder if he'd
like a bone?" she reflected. "There's the one from the
knuckle of the joint. I'll just put this sack inside the kennel,
and go and get it for him."

The fox turned away from the bone, as he had from the
water, and the bandaging was completed in a faint sense of
disappointment because of his flat refusal to accept a single
thing as done in friendliness. They left him chained to

Glen's old kennel with a plate of scraps from lunch, the bone and a dish of water, and Lindsey went out to Lower Naps to fetch Duchess home for the milking.

Twenty minutes later, when she passed the kennel again to get the milking bucket and the water for udder washing, because of Dion's being still away, she saw with sudden pleasure that the plate was perfectly clean, the water dish half empty, and the fox was lying in the doorway gnawing at his bone.

"Do look, Mother!" she said joyfully in the kitchen, where her mother was getting tea ready on the enormous kitchen table. "It's just as if we had Glen again—he's almost the same colour and size, and look at the way he's chewing his bone—exactly the same as darling Glen used to do! Oh, I do hope Mr. Rose doesn't come for him too soon!"

"I hope he does," her mother said. "Think of all the trouble we'll have with Cat and Freyni! And if it comes to that, we've had quite enough trouble with *him* in the short while since we've known him."

Lindsey was filling the washing bucket with warm water at the sink.

"It wasn't any of it his fault," she said. Then, "The nice thing about wearing dungarees at weekends is that when you suddenly have to do a messy job you don't have to take off your skirt and put them on. Oh, potato cakes for tea! Mother darling, how *can* I eat moderately with all this lovely food?"

Mrs. Thornton laughed.

"Why should you eat moderately? *I* don't think you're too heavy."

"No, but I expect Sula does," Lindsey sighed. "It's awful being so tall, you know, because no matter how thin you are, you're bound to be heavy; and it makes your feet so large."

"Eating moderately won't help that!" said Mrs. Thornton, as Lindsey swung her bucket out of the sink. "And it isn't only potato cakes, either!" she added, dropping a final straw to temptation. "There's a chocolate cake —I can't think how I've managed it, with the few eggs we're getting since the massacre—and I've made some Devonshire cream. But I must say I'd feel more like enjoying it myself if Dion were home, and his leg all right and everything. I just can't think how he came to do a thing like that; he usually so sensible with guns."

"Mother darling! Don't *worry!* Even worrying moderately won't help that!"

But it was all very well for Lindsey to talk. As soon as she was settled at her milking in the gathering shadows and quiet of the cow-shed, with the excitement and anxiety about the fox now subsided, she began to worry again about the colt and the Punch Bowl accident. It didn't always work, reminding herself that she had vowed she wouldn't worry, especially when her mind was blank, with nothing urgently occupying it: as when she was in bed, for instance; or as now, with no more to distract her than the slow, comfortable sound of Duchess chewing her cud, or blowing into her manger, clinking her chain; or the frothy double hiss of milk streams plunging into her warm bucket—warm with new milk.

She stared at Phasian, scratching around beside her in the yellow straw, and tried to think of all the things that she might do with her, such as teaching her more tricks or setting her on eggs in the spring, or showing her in the local show. But still her thoughts kept coming back to Chalice, and the car upside down in the Punch Bowl, and Robert Scott, in plaster at the hospital—probably the same hospital where Dion had gone with his father, but there were two or three in Guildford. It was astonishing really that nothing at *all* had been heard from the police . . . if only she could keep jogging along till next Saturday, without continually lapsing into worry, she would know so much more, for by the evening of that day she would have seen Mr. Scott himself . . .

She had come off so badly in this particular lapse of worry that Lindsey was glad to hear the distant roar of the old car, toiling up the steep lane from the village, the creak and clank of the gate at the end of the Old Orchard, and the roaring coming nearer, half a rattle. Then the welcome sound of Peter's voice, hurrying across the yard towards the cow-shed.

144

"I though you would be in here! I say, it's simply super in the hospital, and they let me see some knives. There was a chap there with his arm broken in two places and a girl with something in her ear——"

"How's Dion?" Lindsey interrupted, stripping round the four teats to get the last few drops, which were the richest milk of all.

"Oh, all right. They dug some pellets out, and they said the others didn't matter—they were too deep or something. We've got the stuff for Mother's mole-hills, and some simply wizard cakes for tea——"

"Oh, help!"

"——and Dion's been such a sport coming home; he's worked out a new plan for a simply stunning Muncher-trap. It's rather like the one I made, only Muncher works it by himself. I'll show you when you've finished. Oh—I say, what's happened about the fox?"

"He's in Glen's kennel, and he looks so much like him it makes me feel quite funny. If you're going up that way, will you take the milk and the washing bucket, please, while I feed Chalice and take Duchess back to Lower Naps? I must say, it'll be a lot easier when he's in a field nearer to the house—as well as the ponies, for catching in the mornings."

"Don't you believe it," said Peter, picking up the buckets. "Nothing's ever easy on a farm. As soon as the animals are kept nearer it'll be the winter, and more work haying and feeding and mucking-out. Not that I mind it," he added, as Lindsey unhooked Duchess's chain, "but I must say I wouldn't go so barmy over it as Dion does. Not for a lifetime job, I mean."

With a swing of her fawny-yellow quarters, Duchess passed him at the doorway and went out with all the stately dignity that was natural to her.

"I don't know," Lindsey said, standing on the cow-shed step a moment, watching the cow, and the farmhouse, and the yew tree, and the evening settling down. "At least, as far as this farm goes, sometimes I think it is the loveliest place on earth."

CHAPTER SIXTEEN

Born to Chains

JUST after tea, in the last grey veil of daylight, the fox-shoot came back through Punch Bowl farmyard, and Mr. Morton called at the house to ask after Dion and to report a bag of two dog-foxes and a vixen, not counting Mr. Rose's wounded tame one.

Mrs. Thornton, who was in the kitchen washing up the tea-things, said Dion was doing fine, and should she call him? He was helping Peter make a glider in the sitting-room.

"Oh, no, it doesn't matter, we ought to be getting on. We've mostly got a hundred jobs waiting for us when we get home. Sorry about the accident, Mrs. Thornton—it was my gun did it, you know—but the fool boy rushed out, if you'll excuse my saying it."

Mrs. Thornton said she entirely agreed, it *was* foolish to rush out when men were shooting, and she couldn't think how Dion had come to do it.

"Well, it was the sight of that fox on its chain, of course; silly thing to do, all the same. By the way, tell Dion we called at Rose's place but he said he didn't want the fox now, since he'd got the vixen; and in any case, he said, it was the second time it had slipped him, and he never found it got on very well with his dog, the way the vixen does."

"Oh, dear," said Mrs. Thornton. "How very awkward. It doesn't get on very well with our cats, either. I don't know what we'll do with it."

"Well, I could soon put paid to that, if it's any help, now I'm here with my gun."

"Thank you very much, but I don't think perhaps we ought to have it shot just like that, without asking the children. Oh, dear, and they're sure to say no."

146

She looked across the shadowy garden to the kennel in the yard, where the dog-fox looked more than ever like old Glen, with the light so dim and pearly in the evening. He stood, three-legged, in the doorway of the kennel, with his muzzle lifted westwards to the sunset and the valley, but he was born to chains and kennels and he did not fight his bondage.

"Well, in that case, I'll be getting along back down the lane now. Thank you for the shooting, Mrs. Thornton, and let me know if I can help you with the fox—you know what I mean."

Mrs. Thornton said she would, bade him good night, and went to find her children in the sitting-room.

"Oh, Mother *darling*, your hair is such a sight, I shall never get used to seeing you suddenly come into a room!" said Lindsey, lowering her recorder. "Do you like this tune I've made? Listen—it goes to some words about Chalice— just a minute while I blow my nose."

Mrs. Thornton said, "How on earth you people think I know *what* you want done with my hair, I can't imagine! First, you say it's too long and old-fashioned, and then, when I cut it you say it looks a sight. However, never mind —of course, I'd like to hear your tune, pet."

"Has it never occurred to you, dear Mama," murmured Dion, "to go to a professional hairdresser?"

Mrs. Thornton sighed, looking for her reading glasses on the window-ledge. "I suppose it has, Dion, but it's so far away, and such a *bother*. There's never time enough for all the *necessary* things."

"Shut up everybody, please!" said Lindsey, and she played the tune over while her mother found some mending and a pad and pen to write to Andrea.

"I think it's quite beautiful, darling! It has a sort of wistful lilt, like an old folk-song. You ought to write it down."

"I expect it *is* an old folk-song, really," said Peter, not looking up from the glider, spread in pieces on the sofa, "and she heard it somewhere and forgot it."

"I didn't, and it isn't!" said Lindsey indignantly. "You horrid boy . . . ! Yes, I think I would like to write it down;

147

I'll have to get Mr. Wingfield to help me do it on Friday. Did I tell you, Mother, that he says the vicar says I can go down and practise any day, in daylight? Only not Sundays, of course; and I couldn't go today because of harrowing and the fox and everything. Oh, dear, I do wish we weren't just starting dark evenings again! I'll hardly ever be able to go down till the Christmas holidays."

"And then it'll be awfully cold," said Dion, cutting balsa-wood strips with an old razor blade. "No heating on, in week-days. The church'll be like a tomb."

"Speaking of the fox——" said Mrs. Thornton, having seen an opening.

"Have you noticed," said Peter suddenly, looking up, "how just like Glen he is? Lying there in the old kennel doorway, just the way old Glen used to do. I wonder if foxes get hard-pad distemper?"

"Now *you* shut up!" said Lindsey crossly. "Anyone would think you didn't care at all about poor darling Glen."

"Well!" said Peter huffily. "And didn't I just say how nice it was, the fox's looking like him?"

"No, you didn't. You just said he did look like him, and then went on to reap up hard-pad."

"You mustn't be so sensitive, darling," said her mother, darning tranquilly at a hole in a grey sock of Peter's. "If you keep on letting things hurt you the way you do, you'll always be just a bit unhappy. I don't mean I want you to be hard-boiled, but I do think we have to learn to accept some hard things, because life just is that way."

"Look at me," said Peter, "all the trouble I have with Mr. Muncher—one disappointment after another—and then I've broken my last good strip of balsa I was saving for the tailplane—to say nothing of losing all my mice the way I did last summer; and I don't go around looking like doom."

"Well, do I?" Lindsey's voice was dangerously high.

"Speaking of the fox," said Mrs. Thornton hastily, "I was, a moment ago, but someone interrupted——"

"That was Peter," said Lindsey under her breath.

Mr. Thornton suddenly looked from a book he had been quietly reading, deep in the shabbiest, most comfortable arm-chair.

"Lindsey."

"Sorry, Dad."

"Not like you to tell tales."

There was no answer, so Mrs. Thornton tried again.

"About the fox—Mr. Morton just looked in when I was washing up——"

"How many did they shoot?" asked Dion.

"Two dog-foxes and a vixen, he said; and he asked after you, and he also said they'd called at Mr. Rose's house and Mr. Rose said he couldn't take the fox now he had the new vixen, and that in any case, it hadn't got on well with his dog."

"Oh, yippee!" Peter shouted joyfully. "Then we can keep him! What do they eat, Dion, do you know? Mother, you'll have to order some dog-biscuits again on Monday; I expect he'd like a few of those."

Lindsey said happily, her annoyance forgotten, "I'll tell you what! We ought to ride out to see Mr. Rose ourselves tomorrow, and ask him all about how to care for him. He'll tell us his name, too, and all sorts of things like that."

"We can't keep a pet fox here!" said Mr. Thornton suddenly, looking up again.

"Oh, but *Father!*" said Lindsey.

"Anyone'd think it was a wart-hog," said Peter.

"Well, I ask you, a fox! Isn't that the one thing Dion's been so against? Dead pullets, robbed snares, lanterns by the poultry-arks and all the rest. I'm surprised at you, Dion."

"I only brought him home because he was hurt," Dion said. "But all the same, I don't see why we can't keep him, now he's here and got no home. I think it would be rather fun. And since we haven't had Glen the kennel has looked rather empty. Besides, what else could we do with him?"

"The same as you went out to do this afternoon, my lad."

Mrs. Thornton said, "That's what Mr. Morton suggested. He said now he was here and had his gun with him——"

"*Mother!*" said Lindsey, horrified. "And after you helped to dress his wounds and everything! And you gave him

149

food, too, and a bed and all that—I'd never have believed it of you."

"Believe what, child? I'm only telling you what Mr. Morton said."

"I know; but it's the way you're telling it—as if you really agreed with him."

Peter said, very shocked, "I shouldn't have thought anyone would even think of it! It would be murder, just the same as shooting Vashti or Freyni. He isn't really a *wild* fox, he's just as tame as they are."

"After all," said Dion, "if Mr. Rose can keep a tame fox I don't see any reason why we shouldn't. He seems quite a gentle one, too, for a dog-fox."

"That's probably because he's wounded," said his father.

"Oh, no, Dad! any animal's much fiercer when it's wounded, surely."

"Think of how he *smells!* And supposing he breaks loose; he's done so twice with Mr. Rose," his mother pointed out.

"Where will all your hens and geese be then?" his father said reasonably. "To say nothing of Peter's Mr. Muncher."

"We've got a wonderful new idea for Mr. Muncher," Peter hastened to explain. "We'll probably have him caged, this time tomorrow. Dion thought it all out, coming home from hospital, and old Muncher works it by himself. Shall I tell you how it goes?"

"Oh, not *now*, Peter," said Lindsey, "with all this doom hanging over Dion's fox. Let's get that settled first. It makes me quite awful in my stomach when I'm bothered with suspense."

Dion's fox . . . Dion hadn't thought of it quite like that before, but he supposed she was right; it really was his fox, in a way, since he had rescued it and Mr. Rose disowned it.

"All right," he said, "if he's my fox—and I expect he is— I'll take the risk of keeping him. He can have a stronger chain—one of the calf-tethering ones'd do—and I can go on keeping a lantern by the hens. I expect he'll be just as wary of a light as any wild fox."

"Besides," said Lindsey, "if he ever does break away, I

should think the first thing he'd do would be to go straight back to the valley."

"He might even keep other foxes away," suggested Peter, "while he's there in the kennel."

"Not like a Vixen," said Dion, "attracting all the dog-foxes. And I don't see how anyone can mind his smell when he's out in the kennel."

"It isn't a *nasty* smell," said Lindsey. "Just an ordinary fox-smell."

"Well, since you seem to have settled it all between you, without asking Mother's and my advice," said his father, "it's only fair that you should take the full responsibility. No asking me to buy more poultry if the last survivors go the same way as the others?"

"Of course not, Dad; I said so, only just now."

"And what about Cat and Freyni? We don't want scenes like that every time they set eyes on him."

"They don't bother very much, now he's living in the kennel," said Lindsey. "I expect they think he's sort of Glennish."

"Who's mentioning Glen now?" demanded Peter.

"It wasn't *men*tioning him I minded, you ass!" said Lindsey. "No one ever understands."

Dion jumped up, laying down the balsa strip and razor blade inside the glider box.

"Who's coming down to give him some supper? He can have a crust, can't he, Mother, till we get some proper dog-biscuits? And there's all that skimmed milk in the cellar, he might like a little of that."

"I'll come!" said Lindsey, twisting her recorder into its two pieces and rolling it quickly in the old shantung hand-kerchief.

"Me, of course!" said Peter. "And after that, there's just time before supper to put some snares out; shall we, Dion?"

They were going through the doorway.

"We could, but it's not so easy, doing them by torchlight."

"Oh, but it's much, *much* more exciting! You can always pretend you're poaching, and that it's someone else's land, and frightfully dangerous——"

151

"I suppose you could," said Dion. "I never thought of it."

"And for once," said Lindsey, sniffing the cold dark air outside the back door, "I think I'll come with you."

"Good fellow," said Dion from the larder where he hunted out a thick brown crust. "We'll make a proper trapper of you yet."

"It isn't that," said Lindsey apologetically. "It's the smell of the air—Octobery and frosty—and the quietness, and all the starriness of it."

CHAPTER SEVENTEEN

A Streak of Wild

"FREYNI'S so much better now," said Lindsey, wringing out the dish mop, "you can *see* her getting fatter. She really is fat now, don't you think?"

Peter was laboriously drying for her, one spoon or knife at a time.

"Yes, and smugger than ever. I never saw an animal look so smug as she does."

"It's her mouth that does it," Dión said, coming downstairs from making his bed. "It turns up at the corners."

"And she accentuates her smugness by sitting around in lonely places," Lindsey said, drying her hands at the roller towel. "The way she is now—on the cellar door-step."

Peter said wisely, "That's because the bacon's down there." He dropped the last knife into the knife box, hung up the tea towel and stood in Dion's way by the back door. "You aren't forgetting about the Muncher-trap? You said you'd help me with it first thing after breakfast."

"Gosh, so I did! And I was just going to give the kennel a proper clean-out before we went to see Mr. Rose. Oh, well, it won't take long. Get your trap and bring it out to the Old Orchard. We can see it from the house, in there."

"Oh, golly," said Peter anxiously, hurrying out, "I do hope it does catch him this time. He was *in* the garden this morning, Father said, and he says much more of that and there'll be another rabbit pie."

Lindsey pulled on her jacket, following him. "And not only that—he's been eating Mother's pinks. She was frightfully put out. Especially when she found the lilac branch the fox broke—and that the naptha hadn't stopped the moles. She said there were three more mole-hills, and what with one thing and another she might just as well give up the struggle."

Dion said, "I don't know why she tries, honestly. If it isn't hens and geese getting in, it's the heifers or the ponies or the rabbits or the moles."

"For the same reason that you go on trying to farm, I expect," said Lindsey. "You have just as many handicaps. I think that sort of thing only makes people try harder."

"I dare say you're right, O Wise One! Now what we want is one really fresh cabbage—no, not the weary one you were using yesterday and the day before, Peter—and some string and two sticks."

"As simple as that!" marvelled Lindsey. "I thought from what Peter was saying that it was a perfectly wonderful contrivance."

"All the most wonderful contrivances are simple," Dion said. "Take the wheel—or the lever. Now this stick'll do nicely if we break it in two. Buzz along and find the cabbage, Pete. There are plenty in the kitchen garden. Only a very *small* one, but it must be fresh. We've got to tempt him past all bearing."

Peter raced down the yard, causing Phasian to squawk hysterically in the solitude of her private ark. Lindsey ran to let her out, and the pheasant-bird croodled at her, feathers still ruffled, and then found a crimson fallen leaf from the grape-vine, which she carefully picked up and carried round with pride for half the morning.

"Isn't she *clever*?" Lindsey said, attending to her over-turned water dish. "None of the other fowls would think of doing that. To them a vine-leaf is just a leaf, not something beautiful and nice to play with."

Dion shrugged, knotting a piece of string to the shorter end of his carefully-broken stick.

"You know what I think she is—a little wanting." Then, as an afterthought, "I simply don't know why you're always so much in favour of all the *use*less things, Lin. Badgers and deer; hens that don't lay, plough horses that do a quarter of what a tractor can, yew trees that poison, hedges that harbour rabbits, and a colt that wanders, causing accidents and suchlike."

"You don't *know* he had anything to do with the accident! And what about you and the fox?"

"Oh, well——"

This had taken Dion off guard, rather. It was difficult to think of an answer about the fox, all in a moment like this. But Peter's racing return with the cabbage made a change of subject easy.

"Here you are, Dion! I say, you are standing funnily— does your leg hurt?"

"Not really. It's a bit stiff. Now where's your trap? Bring it along to the orchard and I'll show you how to set it up."

"I know how, of course, after your telling me last night. But I'd rather you did it, the first time."

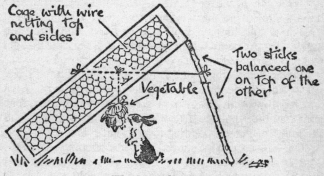

Cage with wire netting top and sides

Two sticks balanced one on top of the other

Vegetable

The Muncher-trap

"What d'you mean, the first time? Once he sets it off, he's caught. Once and for all, I hope."

In the Old Orchard, from which Mr. Muncher hurriedly evacuated on sight of them, they set up the cunning device which they hoped would cause his downfall.

First the trap itself, a simple wire-netting cage about two feet square and nine inches high, open at the bottom but netted over all the sides and the roof. Dion stood it up on edge in order to tie the spare end of his string to the inside of the mesh roof, a little towards one side.

"Now, the cabbage, Peter; it's a bit big—can you take off a few outer leaves? That's better. Now we tie it to the middle of the string, like this. And the other end of the string's already tied to this short stick, see. Now what we

155

do is, we have to prop the cage up at an angle on these two sticks, the short one balanced on the long one. Tricky, this," he said, as the sticks suddenly collapsed, sending the cage down flat with a bump, the cabbage swinging wildly as it went.

"That's what ought to happen when old Muncher munches at the cabbage," he said, starting again. "He pulls the cabbage, the cabbage pulls the string, the string pulls the short stick and the short stick topples off the big one——"

"And down comes the Muncher-trap!" said Peter delightedly.

"With Mr. Muncher inside it," said Lindsey. "And let's hope we're all at the windows to see it. I only hope it doesn't whang him on the head, or make him jump too much. It must be awful, being captured when you thought you had your freedom."

"Better than being shot," Dion said. "There, now, that's got it! Just nicely, too. It won't take much nibbling to fetch that lot down. Oh *Peter!* You great thundering avalanche you!" as the whole contrivance came down with a flop to the touch of Peter's skidding foot. "That's done it."

"Oh, *sorry,* Dion! I slipped on a rotten apple—look!"

"I don't want to look. Now jolly well go into the next field or something—no, it doesn't matter; jolly well set the trap yourself if you knock it down again."

The Muncher-trap was carefully set for the third time in total silence, the cabbage gently vibrating on the taut string between the sticks and the cage top.

"Don't *breathe* on it!" said Peter touchily to Lindsey.

Lindsey jumped up.

"I'm going to catch Nanti. Peter, come and get Sula, if Dion's going to do the kennel first. I say—three of us, two ponies. We'll have to toss up for who stays at home."

"I'll stay," Peter said. "I want to watch my Munchertrap."

"Oh, don't be silly, old chap," said Dion. "He may not even look at it till evening. And even if he does, he'll still be there when we come back."

"Never mind, I'm going to keep my eye on it. I wouldn't

miss seeing him caught for anything, after the trouble I've had over him."

"Well, you're welcome to the notion," Lindsey said. "I'd rather hide in the Punch Bowl, on a morning like this, than do anything else in the world."

"It might be the last day of Indian Summer," Dion said, "and it's school again tomorrow. But anyway, you save us tossing up."

"I'm going to get the ponies," Lindsey said.

Lindsey had long outgrown Sula; and Sula had outgrown her own early high spirits. But still Lindsey really preferred riding her, though Nanti was the peak of excitement and exhilaration to ride, being full of the fire of her Arabian ancestors and tall enough to add a zest that rarely went with riding proper ponies. She wasn't a pony at all, of course, being fifteen hands high, but it was easier to say, "We'll go and catch the ponies," than, "we'll go and catch the pony and the horse," or even "Nanti and Sula."

"I think I shall never really be able to help preferring to ride Sula, so long as she can cope with my awful weight," Lindsey was saying as she and Dion eventually rode away through Yew Tree field to the Punch Bowl. "I expect it's because she was the very first pony, and sort of one of us, and I learnt to ride on her. We've done so many things with her, too."

"Oh, I shouldn't think it's because of any of those things. It's just you—the way you always stick to the things anyone else would throw over." But he grinned at her to show he didn't like her any the less for it.

Through Lower Naps they cantered a little, but Lindsey pulled up soon because of being too heavy for Sula, and through the rest of the heather land they walked sedately. At least Sula did, but Nanti never walked if she could help it, and had continually to be checked for dancing in the treacherous paths among the heather. Lindsey was riding bareback, because of the extra weight a saddle made, and her sandalled feet were brushing through the withered heather-flowers. She still wore her old brown dungarees, and a deep-blue jersey over, but Dion had put on jodhpurs, as he always did for Nanti; she was such a showy little horse

157

that no one felt quite right when riding her in slacks or dungarees.

Sometimes Nanti was positively dangerous in the Punch Bowl, where the paths were very steep and stony. She would swing along down them with her airy dancing step, never looking where she put her feet because her eyes and heart were on the distances. But somehow she never even stumbled, and Lindsey, riding two horse's lengths behind him, thought that Dion looked simply wonderful, the way he swung along as if he and Nanti were a centaur. In fact, this was mostly due to Nanti, and if either she or Andrea had been riding her the effect would have been quite as arresting; for if a person can ride well at all he or she can hardly help looking wonderful on a horse like Nanti. But Lindsey didn't think of this, never having seen herself on Nanti of course, and went on thinking what a stroke of fortune it was to have a brother as splendid as Dion was.

Little Sula plugged stoutly along, her fat grey shoulders warm beneath Lindsey's denim-covered knees. She didn't really have much trouble in keeping up, because for all her display Nanti covered far less ground than one would think; her effort went more into dancing steps and sprung pacing.

Being a Sunday morning Mr. Rose was at home in his garden. On any other day they might have found him out, for his rounds as Game Warden led him far beyond the Punch Bowl.

"Now I'm sorry about that fox," he began, coming down to his fence when he saw the Thorntons approaching. "But you see how I'm fixed, with my own vixen and my dog. And what about that leg, Dion? I hear you got it peppered."

"Yes—it was my fault, of course—nothing much, as you can see, or I wouldn't be riding."

"You needn't be sorry about the fox, Mr. Rose," said Lindsey, slipping down from Sula's back, "because we're keeping him. We're awfully thrilled to have him, and Mother and I have dressed his leg, and we've put him in Glen's old kennel."

"Well, now," said Mr. Rose, "think of that! I wish you well of him, though he never settled down with me, I will

158

say. Funny things, dog-foxes. Wander, you know. And now about that other wanderer of yours, eh?" He looked up suddenly under his eyebrows, smiling knowingly. "You found him all right, so I hear. Not so far from that accident, either! Not that that means anything, eh?" he said, staring with thoughtful satisfaction at his neatly-dug potato plot.

"What we thought was," said Lindsey, rushing in, "that you might be able to tell us some useful things about keeping foxes, since we're going to try to keep this one."

"Their food, for instance," Dion said, patting Nanti's neck. "We've no idea, really, unless it's the same as for dogs. Or mustn't they have any starchy things, like biscuits, at all? It's so difficult to know, with wild creatures. I remember reading in a book about a circus, that the big jungle cats never had to have anything at all but raw meat; yet our cats—same tribe, only domesticated—eat all sorts of other things."

"Freyni likes beetroot," Lindsey said, "and Vashti adores rubber bands, of all the unlikely things. She even eats elastic."

"Natural enough food, rubber, I dare say," said Mr. Rose, leaning on his spade to light his pipe. "Comes from trees."

"Yes, but not natural to *cats*," said Lindsey.

"Well, probably not—but who's to say what they eat when they're living in the jungle? Well, foxes, now! Can't say as I've ever bothered to coddle mine up overmuch. Anything they will eat, I gives 'em. Reckon they know. That old 'un you got, now—he used to fancy jam. Fancied it so strong he'd leave a bone for it, he would. And then again, Trixie—that's my vixen—she won't look at it. All the same, she loves a fry of mushrooms. Neither of 'em bothered with ordinary dog-biscuits, but they'd take to some hound-meal mixed with their meat and gravy, you know."

"That all sounds quite easy," Dion said. "We used to give Glen hound meal and bone broth. He had two meals a day, but the last one was dry biscuit."

Mr. Rose paused for puffing, till his pipe was drawing properly. Lindsey was rubbing Sula's face with the palm of one hand. From the buildings by the cottage came the racket of barking and yapping, but the cottage itself looked the most peaceful place on earth, with the blue wood-smoke circling slowly upwards from its chimney, like travellers' joy against the pine trees.

"Keeps lovely, don't it?" said Mr. Rose contentedly. "Never knew such a wonderful October. Got all sorts of things out in my garden—see my pansies? And all those polyanthuses? Ar, takes a lot to beat a good garden. And the sun! That's like a blessing—truly is."

The smoke from his pipe drifted upwards—a small seedling travellers' joy—and Nanti fretted at her bit, beside the garden gate.

"Well—yes," said Mr. Rose reflectively. "Two meals suit 'em. On the whole, what you want to remember is the kinds of food they eat natural. I dare say you set a few snares sometimes, or walk around with that liddle gun of yours? Well, you can't go wrong if you give him plenty of rabbit, see. Or a pigeon or two. But they're difficult things to shoot, is pigeon, especially with a small-bore gun."

"Raw rabbit?" Dion asked, checking Nanti from trying to circle on the spot.

"Better raw; you can give 'em whole then—fur an' all. But what you really want to watch with the cooked ones is the bones. Never give a cooked bone, they're brittle, see, they splinter. Terrible in a dog's throat. Same with foxes and that, of course."

Lindsey said, "We never even let our cats have cooked bones, except for quite big meat ones. Oh, Mr. Rose, what was the name you called our fox by? We only call him Fox at present, because we wanted to wait till you told us his proper one."

"Well, miss, I always call 'em Toddy. Had a dunna-many foxes in my time, and always called 'em Toddy, 'cepting vixens. I call them Trixie, after my first bitch what I had when I was younger than you are, Dion, by quite a long chalk."

"Toddy," said Lindsey. "I think it's rather nice. Does he answer to it?"

"Oh, ar, they all know Toddy. Same as my three vixens what I've kept have always come for Trixie. I say they

160

come, but mind you, never let a fox go off his lead unless you're with him, and then be sure you know your fox. Gone like a flash they'll be, if you do; for you never quite tame them, you know. There's always a streak of wild in all wild creatures, even if you rear 'em from a baby, same as Toddy was. Come the springtime and the wild will call. Your Toddy, now, he'd always get away if he wanted, chain an' all. Never knew such a fox for his freedom. And that used

Nanti fretted at her bit, beside the garden gate

to worry me, because a loose fox with a chain on is likely as not to get hung up, some place, and die of slow starvation."

"The way he nearly did when we found him," Dion said.

"And if he don't do that," went on Mr. Rose, cleaning his shoes on his spade, "he'll starve a little anyway—I'll telly fer why; you can't hunt, can you, not so well with a great chain chinkling along behind you?"

"Our Toddy is pretty thin," said Lindsey. "But he seems quite well."

"Stands to reason," said Mr. Rose. "Ah, well, I must be

161

seeing to my dinner. No woman in my house, you know. I got to fend for myself; but I don't do so badly and that's a fact. Trixie and Joe and me, we're having rabbit stew today. I better see to it."

"Thank you for telling us so much," Dion said.

"You must come and visit Toddy sometime soon," said Lindsey, jumping back on to Sula.

"Oh, ar, well I might do that. And if you want to know anything else, come along and look me out; I'm generally around at midday and on Sundays. Evenings, too, but they draw in sharpish now, so they do. Be Christmas any day."

Dion and Lindsey heard their own dinner bell as they were riding home through Lower Naps. The bell was fixed upon the farmhouse chimney, for calling home any who were working in the fields, and it was rung by a rope that dangled outside the kitchen door.

"Come on," said Dion. "Sula won't mind a little canter now. We've walked her all the way from Rose's and she's cool and fresh as a daisy."

"She went like a little hunter!" Lindsey said proudly, as they slowed to a walk for the plunging track to the farmyard.

"Positively revelled in it," said Dion, swinging airily to Nanti's airy dancing. "You know, I think these little ponies can carry much more than you imagine."

Peter, on the north lawn, hailed them rather sadly.

"He hasn't been anywhere near it, and I've been around the garden watching all the morning. He hasn't even been in the Old Orchard."

"Cheer up, old man," called Dion, opening the yard gate. "I told you it might be hours and hours."

"Much better to go off and do something," said Lindsey, "and then when you come back you might have a lovely surprise, and find him waiting."

"I don't know about that," said Peter, coming slowly round the corner of the farmhouse. "I'd rather know what's happening—and the cabbage is getting staler every minute."

Lindsey said, "Watching it won't keep it fresh," and followed Dion through the gate.

162

"Oh, by the way," said Peter as an afterthought, "the vicar rang up while you were away, to say that Chalice was found grazing on the cricket green. Some boys took him to the vicarage, because of the stables there, and Mr. Findlay's put him in the loose-box. But he says there's a lawn-mower and a roller in there with him as well as all the cricket things, and six hen coops, so he said perhaps we'd fetch him pretty soon."

"Oh, Hell's *bells!*" said Dion, pulling up Nanti. "Why on earth didn't you tell us at once? And why *couldn't* you have gone down to fetch him? Have the heifers gone too?"

"The heifers are still in Barn field; and I was keeping watch for Mr. Muncher. Besides, the colt's safe enough in the stable."

"What, with all those coops and mowers and things?" said Lindsey, hurriedly dismounting.

"They're Mr. Finlay's anyway. You needn't be so cross about it. I feel bad enough, not catching Mr. Muncher, and Father talking about rabbit pie whenever I see him."

"*Peter!* You little wretch! If they *are* Mr. Findlay's we're even more responsible, and what I meant was that the colt might hurt himself on them!"

Peter shrugged despondently and went towards the kitchen door.

"And I don't believe all that about Father and the rabbit pies, either!" Lindsey shouted from the yard. "I don't believe he's even mentioned it again, since the first time!"

But Peter had disappeared into the kitchen.

CHAPTER EIGHTEEN

Self-Catching Muncher-Trap

THERE wasn't very much left of that Sunday afternoon by the time Lindsey had brought Chalice back from the vicarage down in the village, and Dion had made yet another round of Barn field hedges looking for the gap he had escaped by. This time Peter's help was firmly conscripted and the Muncher-trap remained unwatched among the drift of autumn leaves in the Old Orchard. But when everyone was back again at the farmhouse in the middle of the golden afternoon, there was no sign of Mr. Muncher anywhere, or even that he had been near the orchard.

Peter said he was going off into Hanger field, or probably farther, to discover where he was.

"Well, mind you don't drive him clean away, that's all," said Dion, picking up Toddy's empty dinner dish. "Much better to leave him strictly alone for a bit, if you want him to come nosing round the house again. I say, Lin, Toddy's cleared up every morsel; the dish is clean as a whistle."

"I've often thought about whistles," said Lindsey absently, looking at the colt's stitched place. "I mean, are they really as clean as all that? I should have thought just the opposite; you can't get into the middles of them at all, and think of all the germs from all the people's breaths who've blown them."

"What on earth does it matter? It's only a saying."

"I do wish," said Lindsey wistfully, "that I could afford a really good flute."

Dion said, "Put Chalice back in Barn field and we'll see if he has another shot at it. I'd sooner he got out again today or tonight than any time from Monday to Friday."

"Open the gate, then. You know, his stitched place hardly shows at all now."

"Wonder how he did it?" said Dion, swinging the gate back.

"Yes, I wonder," said Lindsey, feeling hypocritical, because she was as sure she knew the answer as she was sure she knew her own age. She led the colt through the gateway and slipped off his halter. Like lightning, his head came round, and before she could move he had nipped her arm so soundly that she could have cried out with the sudden pain of it.

"Bang him!" said Dion. "The little wretch! He's got to be cured of it."

"I know—he got away too quickly. I wasn't thinking."

The colt was far into the field. Dion said, watching him, "You've only got what you asked for, you know; he's going to be a downright handful soon, unless you start to toughen up to him."

"Yes, I know; but he hadn't done it for so long." Lindsey rubbed her arm, watching the heifers coming down the field. Chalice shook his head, reared once with a sideways turn and got straight down to his grazing. He had had enough excitement for the day. The heifers, swinging their curious poles and jingling their bells, came trotting down to look at him; but it wasn't them he wanted, and with a little snort he strode away.

"Those poles were a really good idea. We'd have been tearing around after the heifers now, if they hadn't had them on," Lindsey said.

"We could take their bells off, I suppose," said Dion. "They don't need both—it's like the hoary tale of the man who wore braces and a belt!"

"Oh, no! I think it would be an awful pity to take them off! I love the sound of them; it reminds me of something I've forgotten years ago and can't remember."

"You are *queer!*" said Dion, grinning at her, and again Lindsey suddenly thought how splendid he looked, with all that dark hair and brownish skin, and his shoulders strong as a man's. It was nice to have a brother like that—not like poor Myrtle Long at school, whose brother had spots, round shoulders, and a skin like writing paper, and couldn't have run a farm to save his life.

165

"We aren't allowed," said Dion, "to use the tractor on a Sunday of course, but we could use Sula in the tub-cart."

"Yes?" Lindsey guessed a job was coming, and wondered just when she was going to fit in a leading lesson for Chalice.

"You know all that bracken Holleybone cut in Nameless field, last week? It's dry enough to cart for bedding."

"Oh, yes, I suppose it would be, with all this Indian Summer weather. You want some help to cart it down?"

"Well," said Dion, grinning again, rather sheepishly. "It's much easier with two."

"All right, I've nothing urgent to do, but I must lead Chalice sometime soon."

"Right! You get Sula and I'll pull the tub-cart from the barn. Honestly, Lin, I just don't know how I'd manage this farm if it wasn't for you!"

"Oh, well——" said Lindsey, turning from watching Chalice and the heifers; and then, because she couldn't think of a single other thing to say, "I'd better get a halter."

The bracken carting took them all the rest of the lovely afternoon, and by five o'clock they were almost drunk with it; the strong, heady smell of sun-dried bracken, the October air like cowslip wine, the rumble in their ears of the tub-cart wheels and all the dreamy-tiredness of hard labour under the sun and on high places. In the yard the little brown stack grew higher; its sides were crisply curling, like the wind on brown peat-water, and all the way up the track from the farmyard lay the faint patteran trail of fallen fronds.

At tea-time Lindsey ate enormously.

"I just can't help it! There shouldn't be such lovely food; and I'm so hungry, even the thought of Sula couldn't make me hold back now."

"The Lord be praised," said Mr. Thornton, passing her the plate of home-made butter. "It does me good to see you eat like a human."

"And still no Mr. Muncher!" said Peter sadly. "I don't know how anyone *can* eat so ravenously, with all this disappointment."

"You're not doing so badly yourself," said Dion. "And

166

anyway, it's really much more *your* disappointment. Ours was when you wouldn't help us fetch the colt from Mr. Findlay's."

"Never mind that now, dear," said Mrs. Thornton, anxious to have tea without an argument. "You'll all of you be clean and ready for church by six o'clock, won't you? We're rather late, today."

"Help!" said Dion. "I've still got the milking."

"You'll just do it," said his father, looking at the clock.

But he almost just didn't, for while Lindsey was clearing away the tea things, looking through the window in the larder, she suddenly saw a thing that made her race to call the others.

"Peter! Dion! Everyone! Do come, Mr. Muncher's in the orchard, and he's hopping round the trap!"

From everywhere the family raced towards the sitting-room, where the big north window commanded a view over all the Old Orchard. Dion had been running hot water into the udder-washing bucket in the kitchen, Peter was feeding his hamsters in the Well House, his mother upstairs attempting to control her hair for church, and Mr. Thornton finishing a letter in his room, in time for the post in the village.

In less than two minutes they were all crowded in the one small spot before the sitting-room north window.

"He's going inside for the cabbage!"

"No, he isn't! He's going round it again."

"That's to make sure it isn't a trap; they're always suspicious."

"Don't be a howling wilderness, Lin! How *can* he make sure it isn't, when it is——"

"He's IN!"

"No, he isn't."

"Oh . . . oh . . . oh!" on notes of descending despair.

"He's going round the back again."

"It's because the cabbage is so *wilted*."

"Can't we put another one—just quickly, while he's around?"

"Oh, Peter, don't be such a wilderness yourself! You'd drive him half across to Kettlebury."

"He IS in! And *look*——"

"The trap's *gone* DOWN!"

"We've caught Mr. Muncher! We've caught Mr. Muncher! I'm going to get him now!"

"Oh, but Peter, what about church? We're late already," his mother's anxious voice went floating after him.

"Oh, but *Mother!* We'll just have to be a bit later——" his voice floated back.

"I'll help," said Lindsey, running after him. "We've just got time, while Dion does the milking. And anyway, better late than never."

And if Mr. Findlay—looking over his spectacles as the Thornton family entered in the middle of the psalms—had realised that the cause was Mr. Muncher, now safely returned to the bosom of his family and eating carrots in the haven of his own cage, perhaps he might have smiled a little as he sang the louder, drowning the noise of their approaching ten shoes upon the aisle.

The following week of school was much more tolerable than Lindsey had dared to expect. For one thing, she began to feel more and more hopeful about the Chalice affair as each day passed without a visit or inquiry from the police. And Chalice himself, after his outbreak on the Sunday afternoon, seemed to have abandoned wandering for a while and grazed demurely with the heifers in Barn field. And then the weather broke, settling into a humdrum dullness and chilliness which made school far less of a burden than if the Indian Summer had continued, with its golden outdoor invitation.

Freyni was so well now that she really *was* quite fat, even in the eyes of others beside Lindsey. And she was smugger than ever, sitting around as she did in solitary places, with her slanting eyes half-shut and mouth upturned at the corners, like a mystic on a mountain or a Buddha in an oriental temple.

Toddy the fox was also a wonderful distraction from anxiety. The strong calf-tethering chain and collar that Dion now used for him had kept him securely at home in his kennel, where he was settling down as well as could be

168

expected. His paw healed quickly, with the healthiness of the wild, and Lindsey saw that he had jam on his crust every day, when she went down after school to feed Chalice, and Phasian, and the hens. He didn't need much exercise now, with his paw still lame, but Dion would take him round the yard on his chain, or into Barn field to look at the heifers in the very early morning before milking. Soon, he would be taking him up to Inner Wood to watch for the young winter corn coming through, or out to Lower Naps with Duchess in the mornings: even, perhaps, into the Punch Bowl to visit his old home and Mr. Rose.

For the first day or two after his capture, Mr. Muncher occupied nearly all of Peter's spare time, even the glider lying neglected and unfinished on the top of the chest of drawers in the boys' bedroom, while Peter worked at strengthening all the weaknesses of Mr. Muncher's cage. He even began adding new refinements, such as a second room in the sleeping quarters, and an extension on the end of the run, until suddenly a new idea struck him.

"I say, Dion," he said one day as they were riding home from school. "You know how easily we caught old Muncher in the self-catching Muncher-trap? Well, I've just been thinking, why not let's try to catch some wild ones with it?"

"Seems quite a notion," Dion agreed, restraining Nanti automatically.

"Yes, doesn't it? I can't imagine why I didn't think of it before, and needing so much rabbit as we do now there's Toddy as well as the cats to feed; and rabbit is *all* of their favourite thing."

"Except perhaps poultry and game, with Toddy!" Dion said dryly.

Peter's notion was quite extraordinarily successful. Anyone looking into Barn field or the Old Orchard, on any early evening after his brain-wave, might have wondered about the propped-up wire-netting cage with a small cabbage dangling round inside it; but if they had chanced to look again, the following morning very early, they would have seen the reason for it. Toddy, Cat and Freyni had rabbit most days after this, and the Thornton family were

169

soon so sick of rabbit in pies and stews and casseroles that Mrs. Thornton had to give up serving them, even in various disguises and most cunning camouflage.

Everyone always looked forward to Saturdays in term time, but Lindsey looked forward to this particular Saturday more than anyone else. Early in the week she had written to Mr. Scott in hospital, asking if she and her brother might visit him on the Saturday afternoon, and saying how much they hoped he was feeling better, and not too bored with bed. Could they, she asked, do any special shopping for him while they were in Guildford? Or was there anything he would like to borrow, such as books or magazines?

His reply was waiting for her on Friday when she came in.

"A letter for you on the dresser, darling," her mother said. "You won't step off the doormat in those muddy shoes, will you? And—good gracious! What's that you've got? Not *another* musical instrument?"

"I've only borrowed it, Mother. It's a piano accordion, and I can't tell you how difficult it was bringing it back on my old bicycle, and over all that stony road. Could you pass my letter, please, because I've still got to shut up Phasian after she's finished her tea, so I don't want to change my shoes."

"But who did you borrow it from, darling? And your organ lesson this evening, too. I'm sure you're dabbling in too many different things. The postmark's Guildford," she added, bringing Lindsey the letter.

"Oh, good! Then it's Mr. Scott, to say whether we can visit him in hospital.—It belongs to a boy at school, but he doesn't mind my borrowing it; and as it's so awfully easy to play, it can't really make much difference to the organ lessons. In any case, they're both keyboard instruments, aren't they."

She lowered the accordion to the floor and leaned against the bridles on the wall to read her letter while her mother went on laying the table for tea.

DEAR LINDSEY,

Thank you very much for your nice letter. I was glad to

170

hear from you, because I had only seen you for a brief moment, with your colt, in the Punch Bowl, but they tell me it was you and that sensible brother of yours who really saved my life: for who would have thought of looking there if you hadn't passed? and it might have been hours before my sister started wondering where I was.

I shall, of course, be delighted to see you both. Saturday afternoon is an excellent time as I don't expect any other visitors then. Your offer of shopping is much appreciated: do please get one of those large blocks of ice-cream (in two colours, I think) and share it with me for tea; we are allowed ice-cream here, as well as guests to tea, which seems a pleasantly human thing in so large and efficient an institution. Perhaps some meringues and éclairs would be a good idea as well; hospital cake is serviceable, but not festive enough for entertaining. (Don't forget it is *my* shopping you are doing, so bring the bill with you.) I could also do with a new toothbrush (very hard) if you have time; my sister forgot it.

Must finish; someone is coming at me with a thermometer. Every few minutes it is washing, temperatures, pulses, meals, medicines, or dressings. We start at five a.m. and are put firmly to sleep at nine.

Yours sincerely,

ROBERT SCOTT.

P.S. Thank you—no books, etc., I am too busy.

"Mother, do read this! Doesn't he sound nice? And isn't everything nice? School finished for another weekend, and Freyni so well and fat she's simply a Snow Mountain; organ tonight, and Guildford tomorrow afternoon and, oh, Mother, even your hair! Did you know its turning up all soft and curly at the ends and looking really *distinguished*?"

"You absurd child!" said Mrs. Thornton, suddenly smiling, and then she read the letter while Lindsey raspberry-jammed a crust for Toddy.

"I didn't know Dion was going with you?" she remarked. 'Mr. Scott seems to think so . . . *Lindsey!* I did say don't go off the mat in those muddy shoes."

"Oh, sorry, Mother! But they aren't really very muddy —I mean, it's dry mud, and I just wanted to get this crust for Toddy." She made giant strides back to the doormat on her heels. "Yes, it's a bit awkward about Dion, isn't it? I just said 'my brother,' but I was thinking about Peter: Dion is always so busy."

"Have you asked him?"

"Well, no; perhaps I might after the organ. He's gone to fetch Duchess down, now; and Peter was setting his rabbit-trap in the gorse in Barn field . . . I wonder what Mr. Scott does, to be so busy in hospital? . . . Mother, do look at Vashti! putting her paw in her bread-and-milk to see if it's hot."

"I know, she always does. Sometimes they're really quite human."

Lindsey suddenly laughed, turning in the back doorway.

"I say, I wonder if they say about us, when they're specially pleased with us, 'Sometimes they're really quite feline!'"

"Or the heifers!" said Peter, appearing on the doorstep. "'Really, my dear, those humans are sometimes almost bovine!' Mother, mother *darling*, how long will tea be? My stomach's so shrunk it's rattling round inside me."

CHAPTER NINETEEN

Dropped Defences

AFTER her organ lesson with Mr. Wingfield, Lindsey took her borrowed accordion down to the cow-shed, where Dion was making a new hay-rack for Duchess ready for her winter nights indoors.

"Father wants the wireless and he says the noise an accordion makes is past believing. I suppose you don't mind if I practise it down here?"

"I shouldn't think I would. Play it and see, and if it's too rowdy I'll tell you. D'you think this is about the right height for Duchess? Nearly always these hay-racks are too high, and the bits fall into the cow's eyes."

Lindsey sat down on the edge of the low manger, the accordion across her knees.

"Looks all right to me. The stable rack's much too high as well, but we can always use hay-nets."

She began to play her chestnut tune, as softly as she could.

"We couldn't use them for the cows," Dion said, between hammering. "Their horns'd get stuck in the mesh. Gosh!" he added suddenly, "what with my hammering and your playing, it's a jolly good thing the cows aren't in now! People who talk about the peace and quiet of the country ought to look in here for a minute."

"But it *looks* quiet and peaceful; the lantern in the rafters and everything."

"Shows up the cobwebs."

Lindsey said, raising her voice over the noise, "Did you know cobwebs are a good thing to have in stables and cow-sheds? It's because they catch flies that would have worried the animals. The blacksmith told me when I took the ponies last time; his place is full of them."

"Much better to use fly-sprays."

Lindsey went on playing without rising to the bait of another argument about old ways versus new.

Dion said, "I'll bet Mother and Dad said something when you brought in that accordion!"

"Mm."

"Nice tune you're playing. Goes with a lilt; what is it?"

"You heard it before, on my recorder. It's the one I made up about the colt."

"How can a tune be *about* anything?"

Lindsey stopped playing because it was too tiresome to keep talking so loudly.

"I mean, it's the words that are about him—about his wandering the way he did."

"Did? You're being jolly hopeful!"

"He hasn't since last Sunday, and today's Friday in the evening."

Dion went on hammering, and the lantern made a shadow of a giant hammering silently beyond him on the wall.

Lindsey stared at the movement of the hammer. This was the time, and the only time, to dare to drop the defences she had held up for so long before the colt; because she must have Dion's help.

Suddenly she said, "It was Chalice who caused the Punch Bowl accident. I've known it all along."

Now it was done. Dion looked at her.

"Well, go on! How do you know?"

"For three reasons. One is where I found him, and one is that I just know, and the other is something much more definite."

"Saying 'I just know' isn't definite at all."

"It is to me. But this one would be to other people, too. Did you know that Mr. Scott's car was the same sort as Mr. Wingfield's is? I remembered afterwards noticing how odd the name looked upside down. Then I had an idea. I measured against my skirt where Chalice's cut came, and when I went down for my organ lesson this evening I measured against Mr. Wingfield's car; it was easy to do it, with him in the church and the car outside. The front mud-guards are exactly the same height as Chalice's cut."

Dion stopped hammering and looked at her.

"Why didn't you say anything before? Not that I think any of it's any proof."

"Because—well, because sometimes I think almost *every*one's against the colt but me; Father because of selling all the animals that aren't absolutely necessary; and you because of his breaking-out and spoiling the hedges and everything; Mother because of his nipping, and she thinks the tradespeople won't come if we don't cure him; even Peter, perhaps, because he was furious about Clover being sold instead of Chalice, when Father said one of them must be. I thought knowing about the accident would be just the last straw."

"Then why are you telling me now?"

"Because I've got to discover if Mr. Scott knows it was Chalice, and I didn't want to put anything down in writing —you know how they use those things in evidence—so I had to arrange to go and see him. I couldn't very well, alone, at my age. I don't suppose I'd even be allowed. And now Mr. Scott has asked us both to tea. Look, here's his letter."

Dion leaned against the stall-partition to read it, and Lindsey started playing again, to take her mind off the suspicion that she was doing the wrong thing in telling Dion about the colt.

"I dare say I could manage it." He folded up the letter and pushed it back inside its envelope. "I've got to do some shopping tomorrow—I want some wellingtons, a whitewash brush, and a haircut, and it may as well be Guildford as Godalming. In fact, come to think of it, it'll have to be; because I'm due to have an eye-test."

"Oh, good!" Lindsey sounded very relieved. "I'm glad it needn't be Peter, because though he's all right in the ordinary way, you never know what he's going to say."

"If it comes to that, what are *you* going to say?"

"Oh, help—how do I know till I say it? I mean, I know what I want to find out, of course; I've just got to know what Mr. Scott told the police—they must have asked him why the car ran off the road. I simply can't bear all this suspense about what is going to happen to Chalice. And the other thing is that I think we ought to thank him; it's the least we

175

can do, when you think he's where he is for Chalice's sake. He could easily have run him down and killed or maimed him, and been perfectly all right himself. You can't let people risk their lives for your colt and not do a single thing about it."

Dion stood back to look at the nearly-finished hay-rack.

"I don't see how you can do that without telling him you know it *was* the colt."

"I know. Oh, dear, what an endless complication life is! Though I must say it sometimes isn't half so complicated as you think it's going to be. Telling you about Chalice, for instance: I took days to make up my mind about that, because I was sure it would only turn you right against him; and it can't have, or you wouldn't be coming tomorrow."

"Why should it have?" Dion was hunting in the manger for a dropped nail. "You don't turn against someone because you know they're in a jam. You try to get them out of it, I should have thought. If Chalice is really in such a jam as you make out, he'll need all the help there is to get him out."

"Honestly," said Lindsey, staring vaguely at her shoes, "I sometimes wonder if I shall *ever* learn much about human nature. No one ever does just what you expect them to—least of all oneself."

Dion laughed, found his nail and put it in his pocket.

"That's the whole trouble with you! Crossing bridges before they've even been built. Come on, let's look at Toddy before supper. There's just time."

CHAPTER TWENTY

Time Going So Fast

IN Guildford the next day, the results of Dion's eye-test were not very encouraging. There was little improvement to report, the oculist said, and he could only repeat what he had said before: that Dion must rest more, for people burning candles at both ends simply could not hope for a cure.

"Give me an idea of your usual day's work," he said "including the times you get up and go to bed."

It did seem a lot, listed out like that: the early rising for milking Duchess and for seeing to all the other creatures in his charge; the long day at school; the journeys backwards and forwards; the homework and farmwork in the evenings. He didn't mention the tramping after animals wandering in the Punch Bowl and the valley, but that had happened fairly often too, just lately. And then at various special seasons, such as haying and harvest and ploughing, the work could mount to a pitch that would have been enough without any school at all.

"It won't do, you know; you've got to cut it somewhere, or you'll be wearing glasses all your life," the oculist said. "And that's putting it mildly. Things could really get very much worse."

Afterwards, walking on along the High Street to finish Mr. Scott's shopping, Lindsey forgot her anxiety about Chalice for a while because of the new worry about Dion.

"I know what we can do! I can milk—well, what's against me doing the early morning one? That would be one thing less, and it won't hurt me to get up half an hour earlier. I always enjoy it, once I'm up, anyway. And another thing is the school journey; well, Peter and I can bicycle on alternate days instead of once in three days, then you needn't bicycle at all, because that way leaves Nanti for you every time."

"Oh, rot—but thanks all the same, There's a chemist just down here for Mr. Scott's toothbrush; and don't forget he wants a very hard one."

"It isn't rot! And if you weren't so proud that you couldn't see it, you'd know it wasn't rot. Why shouldn't we share the work out? It's better than having to let things go, or spoiling your sight for ever."

"I should have thought the reason was obvious. I started all this farming and I ought to see it through."

"But that's just what I meant when I said you were proud. It *is* being proud, not to let anyone help you when you need it."

"All right; even if it is, I still don't want anyone's help— at least not with my own jobs. But this is no place to stand arguing; you're blocking the doorway and we'll be late at the hospital if we don't get a move on now."

They were late, but only a few minutes; and they had all the shopping—including four peaches which were Lindsey's own idea and not on the list—and a fife which she had bought with several weeks' savings while Dion had been having his hair cut.

Mr. Scott was in a small private ward, much to Lindsey's relief, because it was bad enough introducing yourself to a stranger without having rows of interested spectators watching your embarrassment; to say nothing of sudden lulls in the hum of general conversation when every word of your solitary voice was carried round the silent ward.

A first impression with both Dion and Lindsey was the astonishing brownness and aliveness of the patient. Somehow, after seeing him limp and unconscious in torchlight, they had both expected to find him pale and rather listless. Everything about him expressed life and vigour and ability. Seeing them in the doorway, he swept together the piles of papers which were all over his bed and put them on to the table, among the fruit and flowers and books that already crowded it.

"Hullo! We meet again in rather more comfortable circumstances than the last time! There are two chairs somewhere, probably both full of books—just dump them on the floor."

Except for the plaster cast jacket round his ribs one might have thought he was only in bed for his own amusement.

"We've got your toothbrush and things," Lindsey said, fishing in her basket. "And Mother sent some butter, and some eggs, and a jar of cream."

"I hope they'll let you have them, sir," said Dion, unloading the chairs. "She said she was sure they would."

"They will," said Mr. Scott. "I don't stand any nonsense. You just have to be very firm with the nursing staff, and you get on fine. Please thank your mother very much—no, I'll write a note before you go, and thank her myself. She must be very nice."

"Oh, she is!" said Lindsey, fishing out the peaches. "And these are from us. She's not the strict sort, you know—at least not often—and she's frightfully absent-minded, but she never minds being teased about it. What shall I do with the ice-cream? It's getitng rather runny; we forgot to bring a lot of paper to wrap it in, and the shop didn't find us very much."

"Better eat it, I should think. Tea will be here in a few minutes anyway; everything in hospital is about three hours earlier than it is anywhere else. I hope you've got all the bills?"

Dion said, "We didn't get one for the ice-cream, of course, or for the cakes and things. But we jotted it all down on my wellington parcel."

"Sensible idea. Now I haven't any spoons at the moment, but I've got a fruit-knife; we can cut it up with that, and just eat the lumps in pieces of paper, shall we? I've got reams of it around. It's music-paper, I'm afraid, but quite clean."

"So that's what you were so busy at!" Lindsey said. "I can't think why, but music is the last thing I should have thought about."

Mr. Scott laughed. "Did you think they all had beards and long hair?"

Dion was tearing the shopping-account from his wellington parcel paper. He said, "It's because she's cracked about music herself, sir, that she can't realise anybody else might be."

"Oh, I see," said Mr. Scott wisely, dividing the ice-cream into three. "As when people have an operation, or get married, or win a first prize—they think it's so extraordinary it can't possibly have happened to anyone else."

Lindsey began to say, "No, not at all like that really——" but just then the tea came in, and the ward maid couldn't find a place to put the tray, and everything else was forgotten in renewed clearance efforts. Then there was the eating, and it is always so unsatisfactory trying to talk much at the same time, but after the last éclair was eaten Mr. Scott went on where he had left off.

"What sort of music? I mean, what do you play?"

"I suppose the recorder, really," Lindsey said, after a moment's thought. "But I like to try other things, too."

"Too many things," Dion said. "We all keep telling her."

"Only the organ, and an accordion I've borrowed, and the violin at school."

"And what's that thing in your basket?" said Mr. Scott. "Another recorder?" His practised eye was considering an object sticking up beside the handle.

Lindsey looked at it.

"Well, no—it's a fife. I just bought it. I——"

"Lindsey!" said Dion. "While I was having my hair cut! What *will* Mother and Dad say? I shouldn't be surprised if they stop the organ lessons when they see that."

"I can't very much help what they say now, can I? I'd really been saving for a flute," she added wistfully, "but it's simply shocking, what they cost. I'd never be able to afford one if I saved up for all my life."

"What do you play, sir?" Dion asked, wondering whether Lindsey was ever going to get round to the question of the colt before they had to leave.

"Like Lindsey—all sorts of things. I'm a director of music at a boarding school: sounds dull to you, I expect, but it can be quite exciting. Then I sometimes write music, too. That's what I've been doing in here."

"That's like Lindsey, too," said Dion unexpectedly, and to Lindsey's annoyance. "She's made up rather a nice thing; a sort of song about our colt."

180

"The colt I saw you with in the Punch Bowl?"

"Yes," Lindsey said rather miserably. "But it's only the words that are about him, of course. And the tune isn't as good as Dion says. He just isn't musical, you see."

"Play it," said Mr. Scott commandingly, and Lindsey suddenly saw what he meant about handling the nursing staff; the determined voice, combined with a smile of exceptional charm, was irresistible.

"What, here? But what on?"

"What did you buy a fife for? Stirring the hen food?"

"But I can't play it yet; I haven't even tried."

"Now's the time, then. Never let the ground grow under your feet, as a vague friend of mine says. It's pretty much the same as a recorder, you know, only you have to blow a lot harder."

Leaning over the side of his bed he reached the fife from the basket and unwrapped it.

"Not an awfully good one, is it?"

"I can't afford an awfully good one."

"Well, never mind. Here you are. All I really want is to hear the tune; I'm very interested in tunes, there are so few good ones nowadays, you know. You can whistle it if you'd rather."

"I can't whistle when anyone's listening; it doesn't come."

She took the fife, frowned deeply in concentration, took a breath and began to blow. But nothing happened at all except a blowing sound. Dion suddenly began laughing.

"Perhaps there's a spider in it, like the time when your recorder did the same. Shake it and see."

"It isn't that; she isn't blowing hard enough," Mr. Scott said. "You have to blow amazingly hard with a fife."

Lindsey tried again, getting very red in the face with the effort, and a tiny forlorn squeak came out.

"That's better," said Mr. Scott approvingly. "Now, a little harder still."

The squeak went up into a sad expiring wail: a passing nurse opened the door and popped her head round.

"Everything all right, Mr. Scott?"

Dion swallowed back a great gale of laughter, but Mr. Scott said solemnly, "Quite all right, thank you, nurse:

don't let me keep you!" And the white-capped head bobbed away again.

"Now," said Mr. Scott, radiating energy in all directions, "we shall have it next time. A long deep breath, and a great gusty blow."

But Lindsey was laughing now, and it was a long time before the chestnut colt tune wavered surely enough from the fife for Mr. Scott to note it down on a sheet of music-paper from the table.

And still no one had said anything to help clear up the mystery of the colt, and now the nurse was at the door again and saying it was time for visitors to go.

"Yes, certainly nurse; I shan't be more than another half-hour or so. Do your best to see we aren't disturbed too often, won't you? There's a jewel."

Raising her eyebrows despairingly the nurse vanished again.

"If only she doesn't fetch sister," said Mr. Scott, "we'll be all right. Now just run through that last line again, Lindsey. I'm not sure about the second bar. Help yourself to the grapes, Dion, if you're feeling bored with all this."

Time galloped on. Lindsey, carried away with all the excitement of the new instrument, the tune, and the astonishing life and vigour of the patient, was still wretchedly aware that soon they simply must go, and she would never have found out the vital thing she had come for.

"That's fine! I've got it down beautifully now. Dion, you're right, it's not a bad tune at all. In fact, it's a pretty good one. I wish I had you in one of my classes, Lindsey; you ought to see some of the pudding brains I do have; no more music in them than there is jam in a hospital dough-nut. Now the words; they mean much more to a song, you know, than most people think. Here's a clean sheet of paper for you to write them on. Did you make them up?"

Lindsey said, "Yes, mostly while I was washing-up dishes," and started writing out the lines. "There's only one verse."

Time went galloping on, and now the tune had to be played again and set properly to the words.

"If that really is the time, sir, we'll have to be going," Dion said at last, looking at a little clock on the mantel-piece. "I've got the milking to do when we get back; and the buses only go once an hour."

Lindsey shot a last despairing glance at Dion, but though he would have helped her out of all other kinds of fix, he was no hand at delicate and diplomatic inquiry. If she couldn't ask her own questions then they just wouldn't be asked at all. He was standing up now and putting the pile of books back on his chair, and Robert Scott was rushing off his thank-you note to Mrs. Thornton for the butter, eggs and cream. Lindsey could have died of shame, to think that she had come all this way for Chalice's sake, and had been gaily laughing and playing her fife instead of finding out what might be threatening him. Now it was plainly too late, too late altogether. Dion was shaking hands with Mr. Scott, and now she was doing the same herself and putting his note in her pocket, and that nurse was at the door again. And the next thing was that they were walking down the long white corridor to the hospital front door, and then they were out in the street again, and the autumn dusk was already falling round the roofs, and a few shop windows were lit displaying cakes and gowns and pottery.

"You *are* a silly old ass, really Lin!"

"I know, don't rub it in!"

"All this way, and now you still don't know."

"You don't think I'm not wretched about it myself, do you? You just can't realise how impossible it is, when you're trying to think what to say and everything, and the time going so fast."

Dion said nothing, threading along the pavement through the Saturday afternoon shopping crowds.

"And that isn't the only thing either," said Lindsey miserably when they came to a clearer stretch of pavement. "I didn't even thank him."

"Well, honestly," said Dion, picking up speed before the crowd thickened again, "I don't see how you could."

CHAPTER TWENTY-ONE

By Express Private Post

ON Sunday morning Lindsey got up very early. The only thing to do with a state of anxiety is to work or play so hard that you haven't time to think about it, and it was a very good day to practise this because of her resolution to take on more of Dion's jobs. She began with the early milking, and was so dogged about it that Dion suddenly gave up arguing about his personal responsibilities and went off with Vashti and the four-ten. By the time he got back she had cleaned out the cow-shed, too, fed Chalice his oats and chaff—which were his special privilege for building bone and muscle—and taken Duchess back to Lower Naps.

"I've got a rabbit for Toddy. Peter can set up his Muncher-trap to get another if you want one for the cats."

Lindsey was inside Phasian's ark, renewing water and grit and her small ration from the hen food.

"Oh, good. Is Cat there? Don't let her into the ark, but could you just come inside and have a look at Phasian? I do hope she isn't ill or anything—look, she's sort of sitting huddled in a corner, and she won't come out for her breakfast, the way she usually does."

Stooping along under the low roof of the ark, Dion squatted on his heels to peer inside the sleeping quarters.

"Hm; well, I don't know. If she were any other hen I'd think she might be laying—or going broody."

"I say, I never thought of that! Perhaps she *is* laying!"

"I shouldn't think so," Dion said. "Not she. But, of course, you never know. Anything's possible, or so we're always being told. Did you remember to put that stuff on Duchess's udder? I think she must have scratched it on a bramble."

"Yes, and I put a new salt-stick out for her, too; the old one fell to pieces in the manger when she licked it."

184

"Come and see Toddy with his rabbit," Dion said, backing out into the yard again. "We can't help Phasian by crowding round and staring at her."

At breakfast Peter was bursting to tell everyone about the *two* rabbits he had found in his Muncher-trap that morning.

"I mean, *two*," he said. "Both together. That's twice as many as Dion got, going out with the gun and Vashti. And I didn't have to do anything at all except set the trap properly."

"Well, you needn't sound so smug about it," Dion said, sugaring his porridge.

"I don't see why not; I *feel* smug. I feel so smug I could outsmug Freyni."

"Little horror!" said his father, looking over the top of his coffee.

"You couldn't!" Lindsey said. "You couldn't possibly; my cat is simply unoutsmugable."

"I'm writing to Andrea this morning," Mrs. Thornton said, "so if anyone can manage a note to put in with mine, please let me have it in good time for the post. And don't forget, all the house jobs must be done before anyone goes off outside."

"Oh, but Mother!—I must just have a quick look at Phasian! She wouldn't come out for her breakfast."

"And I absolutely *must* feed old Muncher. I haven't done him yet because when I saw the two rabbits in my trap, from my window, I just rushed straight up to get them. After all, I knew how glad you'd be to have two rabbits for the cats, even if we don't like them any more ourselves."

"Only me, that's perfect!" began Dion, with a hand on his chest; then, "Oh, heck, no! I forgot Toddy. I say, I'm awfully sorry, Mother darling, but I've got to go and change the dressing on his paw. It was half off when I took him his rabbit."

"I don't think I ought to allow any of it," said Mrs. Thornton. "If I were some mothers, you know I wouldn't."

"Of course you wouldn't, dear Mama," Dion said, "so what a good thing it is that you aren't some mothers."

185

"You must all come back the minute you've looked at these creatures."

"The minute!" agreed Lindsey on the doorstep.

After they were gone, Mrs. Thornton suddenly stopped in the middle of clearing the table and said, "George, you know Lindsey did the milking this morning? And she was cleaning out the cow-shed, too, when I looked out later. You know, I wonder if the oculist told Dion he had to rest more?"

"He said remarkably little about it, when they came in."

"Yes, and it would be just like Lindsey to throw herself into the breach. I only hope she isn't the next one to crock up. You know, sometimes I think the work is really getting too much for them. It was different when we had Holley-bone."

"A thing I've been thinking lately myself," said Mr. Thornton, stacking his cup and saucer on his plate, "is that I'm not getting enough outdoor exercise. Does it take very long to learn to milk? And anyone can fetch a cow in from a field."

There was a sudden rush of footsteps outside, and Lindsey appeared on the doorstep.

"Mother! Father! I say, what do you think? Would you believe it, but Phasian has just laid an egg!"

She held it up between finger and thumb, dancing round the table with it.

"Let me look, darling! Stand still a moment."

"It isn't very big," her father said. "It isn't any bigger than a bantam's egg."

"But it's only her first one, after all that nervous break-down and everything, Dad! You can't expect her to lay ostrich eggs, when after all she's only convalescent."

"It's rather a beautiful egg," her mother said, taking it into her hand. "All brown with little white speckles."

"Like Phasian," said Lindsey proudly. "You would expect a beautiful hen to lay beautiful eggs. It isn't always *size* that counts. And anyway I expect she'll lay much bigger ones when she really gets going."

Another rush of feet along the path outside announced Peter.

"Mother! Dad! I say, would you believe it, Mr. Muncher's got out again! I wouldn't have thought it *possible*."

"Oh, Peter old chap, I am so sorry!" said his mother.

"Don't you let him get into the garden again, or mark my words——" began his father.

"Yes, I know, Dad, he won't. And you needn't really be as sorry as all that, Mother dear, because I can easily catch him again now, with my Muncher-trap. I'm going to set it up at once——"

"No, you aren't, Peter; you're going to make your bed and do the sitting-room carpet first, before you do anything else at all."

"Oh, Mother!"

"No arguing," said his father. "The sooner you get it done, the sooner you'll be out. And mind you do under the sofa. When I pushed it back yesterday I found half a comb, a water-pistol and a whole colony of crumbs."

"Now, look!" said Lindsey, turning round from the dresser where she had been writing on her egg. "It's a really literary egg now—did you know Phasian had laid an egg, Peter?—I've written 'Phasian. Her egg. First after her breakdown. Phasian laid it. Not to be cooked, please.' And the date."

"What, all that on that tidgy egg?" Peter marvelled.

"It isn't a tidgy egg! And first ones are often a bit small. Don't you think it's a beautiful colour? Like snowflakes on frozen coffee."

"Mm. I suppose any egg's worth having, now we get so few," Peter said, and stumped upstairs.

Lindsey attacked the washing-up with great energy, refusing to think about Mr. Scott and his accident, or what her parents had said about spending all her money on a fife ("Really, Lindsey, this is getting past a joke"), and afterwards she wrote a hasty note, with illustrations, for Andrea, and then she caught the colt and took him for a leading lesson.

Peter had lugged his Muncher-trap down from the gorse in Barn field and was setting it up again under the apple trees in the Old Orchard, and Dion was walking Toddy

187

round the track to look at the newly-sown and harrowed Inner Wood. It was the first really sunny and tranquil day since the Indian Summer interlude, and no one wanted to be indoors.

Up the track from the gate came a young woman on a bicycle, and Lindsey, leading Chalice, met the bicycle half-way, beside the Swing Tree.

"Good morning! This is Punchbowl Farm, isn't it? I thought I was never going to find it."

"Yes, do you want to see my father?" asked Lindsey, wondering if this was an author in search of an artist, or what?

"No, I have a letter I promised to deliver. I'm a nurse at the hospital in Guildford, and a patient of mine asked me to deliver this to Miss Lindsey Thornton, as he said I should be passing quite near the farm, and it was urgent. I must say, his idea of 'quite near' isn't mine! Anyway, here it is. Would you give it to her, please? He was very particular about her having it this morning."

"Oh, thank you! I am Lindsey Thornton. I expect it's from Mr. Scott. Stand *still* a minute, Chalice!—he's very young you see—I mean Chalice is; perhaps I'd better take him back, if you'll excuse me. Thank you very much for bringing the letter; whatever can it be about?"

"I expect you'll soon know," said the nurse. "Well, I'll be getting along. I've got to get to Hindhead before lunch."

Lindsey shoved the letter into her pocket, knowing it would be hopeless trying to read it with Chalice dancing on the end of his halter-rope. She led him back up the track, under the breaking wave of golden branches now dropping their leaves about her head, and let him go again in Barn field with the heifers.

Sitting on the gate—at the hinge-end, because it was the strongest—she tore open the envelope and read.

DEAR LINDSEY,

You don't teach two hundred young people for eight years without learning something about them, so you will forgive me for knowing why you came to see me yesterday.

It was bad luck, not having time to get round to it, but as it was largely my fault for starting you off on the fife and your tune, I am now making up for it by sending you by express private post all the details (I hope) that you require. (A nurse is having a day off, and I have persuaded her that the Devil's Punch Bowl is a place everyone must see before they die, and well worth a bicycle ride from Guildford. She thinks she is going to be near enough to drop this letter in as she passes.)

Now to the settling of your so excellent mind:

Yes, of course, I know it was your colt on the road: I saw you with him after I came round; but luckily someone said you were your brother's sister before I was asked any questions; so naturally, I was careful not to say anything to the police or anyone else that might have cast suspicion on him. One doesn't endanger the animals of friends and rescuers, does one?

I have, by the way, suggested to the police that whatever it was that rose in front of me was about the size and colour of the wild deer which I understand are living in the Punch Bowl. In a shifting fog, of course, no one can be certain, and musicians are often very vague.

My car was fully insured, and I am enjoying my enforced rest after years without a holiday, so don't worry!

Your tune is really much better than you have any idea. It may be a flash in the pan, of course, and not the first effort of a future famous composer, but it is almost perfect in its own way and, if you will let me handle it for you, it should make you quite a useful little sum of money. You wouldn't be averse to having it broadcast, I expect? Let me know what you think and we can discuss it more fully; probably at another tea-party, either here in hospital or at my sister's flat in London.

Yours, very sincerely,

ROBERT SCOTT.

P.S. The peaches were delicious, and the toothbrush most excellently hard.

Afterthought: By the way, my sister says there is really no room at all for my piano in her flat, now she

189

has bought a new bookcase. I wondered if you'd like to
keep it aired for me at Punchbowl Farm, until such
distant day as I have a house or flat of my own?

R.S.

For a few minutes Lindsey went on sitting on the gate,
staring hard at nothing in particular. Then, with a sudden
leap, she catapulted herself into the yard and went racing
into the house.

"Mother, Mother darling! Isn't it a wonderful day? Isn't
everything absolutely perfect? Where's Dion? Still out with
Toddy? I simply must find him!"

Tearing out again she went dancing up the track to Inner
Wood, where Dion and the dog-fox stood on the corner
looking out across the field.

"Dion! It's all right—*every*thing's all right! Freyni, and
Phasian, and Mother's hair, and now Chalice and my tune
and Mr. Scott, and even a piano! Look, here's his letter; he
sent it with a nurse. I say, isn't it simply marvellous the way
he manages the nursing staff? How much d'you suppose
my tune will earn? Enough to have Holleybone every day
again, until your eyes get better? And proper fences built?
Isn't absolutely everything all right? It simply couldn't be
righter."

"Well, give me half a chance to finish reading it . . . My
word, Lin, you look like being famous! Though what Mother
and Dad are going to say about you starting yet another
instrument, I wouldn't like to guess. And isn't it good about
Chalice? We've really got to do something to make sure he
doesn't go up there again. And don't be an ass; if you earn
any money it's for you yourself—though I don't expect it'll
be as much as you think, anyway."

They were walking back to the house, and Toddy was
jumping on the end of his chain, infected by Lindsey's high
excitement.

"I don't want it for myself, I only want to keep Chalice,
and to have you well and everything. Can I lead Toddy,
please? I hardly ever do."

At the end of the field Dion suddenly grinned, looking
over the hedge into the Old Orchard.

190

"I don't know what Peter would say about everything being all right; just look at old Muncher!"

They stood and stared over the hedge, the dog-fox worrying at his chain around her legs. Peter was just visible, hiding in the tall brown bracken fronds, and Mr. Muncher lolloped carelessly around the succulently-baited Munchertrap.

"He knows how to bait it nowadays," Dion said. "Practice makes perfect."

"It looks like a mixed salad hanging there," Lindsey said. "I wonder if Mother knows?"

Suddenly Toddy saw the piebald rabbit through the hedge and made a rush. The chain slipped through Lindsey's unwary fingers, and the fox was a red streak through the orchard.

"Catch him, Peter!" Dion yelled, as Mr. Muncher vanished into a burrow under the walnut tree.

"You doddering great lunatics!" shouted Peter, shaking his fist. "I'd nearly got him, too." But he caught Toddy all the same, and then suddenly calmed down. "It doesn't really matter, I suppose. It's awfully easy to get him again now. But it *is* maddening, nearly having him, and then seeing him chivvied away."

"It was my fault," Lindsey said. "I'm awfully sorry, but the chain just slipped straight through my fingers. I wasn't expecting him to pull like that."

"I'll help you set it up again," Dion said. "And then, if you like, I'll have a look at his cage."

Lindsey said, "Shall I put Toddy in the kennel, then? I'm going down; I want to write a note and catch the post with it."

In the house she wrote :]

Dear Mr. Scott,

Thank you! Thank you very much indeed! Must catch post, more later.

Yours sincerely,
Lindsey.

"And now I've thanked him, too!" she said to herself, running down the track to the post with her letter and the family one to Andrea. "Everything really is all right—or as nearly so as it ever is in real life."

THE END